LOCKED AND LOADED FOR JUSTICE

RENA KOONTZ

RENA KOONTZ

Published in the United States of America by

Rena Koontz

1181 S. Sumter Blvd. #143

North Port, FL. 34287

ISBN: 978-1-7322709-8-5

renakoontz.com

LOCKED AND LOADED FOR JUSTICE
SAVING GIA

BY

RENA KOONTZ

Dedicated to my sister, Georgianna ——
because my books always made you proud.

1

This week's trip into hell was over.

Blake Matthews tightened the straps on his daughter's car seat, her sweet face wet with tears, her tiny chin quivering, her dark eyes downcast. How much longer was the court going to torture her like this? How much longer was he going to allow it? The title "Family Court" was laughable. The people running this show didn't have the faintest idea what "family" meant. If they did, they wouldn't be ripping his family apart.

He dropped a kiss on top of Gia's head and slammed the door. He could use a drink right now. Just to take the edge off. His mouth watered contemplating it. First things first. Get the hell away from this place.

The hour visit with Gia's mother, his ex-wife, was excruciating. Feeling Gia tremble in his arms while Lynne tried to cajole her closer, seeing those long red fingernails come through the air at them both, sensing his daughter recoil—it was too much. How had he ever loved that woman?

He jammed his foot to the gas pedal. The tires screeched his departure from the parking lot.

"We'll be home shortly, Peanut. Noreen is waiting for us."
He needed the woman's arms around him more than a scotch.
More than Gia needed her.

No response from his little ray of sunshine. It crushed him.
These visits left his baby girl morose. Him too. He practically
tasted that scotch.

"It'll be okay, sweetheart. Daddy will figure out a way to
fix it."

How, he didn't know. He had the chance last year. He
should have killed her mother then.

THE DOOR to Blake's truck slammed in the driveway with a bang
as loud as a cannon shot.

Noreen laid her book aside, straightened her position on
the chaise lounge to support her leg, and gingerly braced
herself against a pillow. The burns on her back and arms had
healed, but the pain remained.

Sparkly rainbow-colored sandals pounded across the
kitchen tile and the hinges on the screen door squealed when
Argia shoved through it, hurling herself onto Noreen's lap.

"Weenieeeee." The trembling child buried her face in her
chest, and rounded fists bunched her cotton shirt into a sweaty
ball. Despite the circumstances, the nickname made her smile.
Gia couldn't pronounce the r-w combination in her name at
first, and instead started calling her Weenie. The pet name
stuck. She wrapped her arms tight around Argia and rocked
slowly from side to side.

"Shh, it's okay, honey. You're home now. It's okay."

They rode this emotional roller coaster every time Argia
returned from a court-ordered visit with her mother, sobbing,
shaking, and clinging to Noreen's shirt until she was cried out.
There'd be a few hours of silence with Argia simply nodding

yes or no or not responding at all. No amount of cajoling or bribery coaxed her out of her self-imposed muteness unless her father worked his special magic, employed his "twofer" kisses, and shared his soulful gaze with his daughter.

But these visits took their toll on Blake too. Even over Argia's sobs, chunks of ice dropping from the icemaker into his glass reverberated out to the patio. Next, he'd walk to the liquor cabinet.

She eyed the screen door while she rocked Argia, whispering comforting words to reassure her that her daddy loved her, and she loved her, and everything would be better soon. Would it?

Blake needed the same assurances but cradling him in her arms like a child wasn't the answer. She was at a loss as to how to help him. Why didn't he walk out onto the back deck? Gia needed him.

Argia's outburst subsided to sniffles, her eyes wide and staring at Noreen. The child spoke volumes through those expressive chocolate eyes. She harbored a fear no six-year-old should have to bear. A child shouldn't be so afraid of its mother.

Finally, the hinges squeaked and Blake strolled out, the alcohol in the tumbler already half consumed. He dragged a chair close to them, leaned over to drop a scotch-laced kiss on Noreen's mouth and sat, taking a hefty swallow before setting his now empty glass on the table. When he opened both hands and gestured with his fingers, Argia crawled from her lap to the security of her father's arms, settling her beloved stuffed animals against his chest and nestling her head in the crook of his arm. In seconds, her eyes closed and her breathing evened.

There was no point in asking how the visit with his ex-wife had gone. It always caused Argia to have nightmares and Blake to drink. He'd been doing that a lot more lately.

She laid her hand over his on the chair's arm. "Can I get you anything?"

His gaze at her lacked focus. Like his daughter, Blake could communicate his feelings through his gunmetal gray eyes. He was lost.

"Another drink would help. But I don't suppose that's what you meant. And you wouldn't be happy about that."

She smiled without feeling any joy. "We both know that won't help."

This was a discussion they'd exhausted over the last four weeks. Since his ex-wife's release from a psychiatric hospital to a halfway house designed to transition her back to self-sufficiency, the happy ride through daily life that she and Blake shared was jarring, like a car that suddenly gets a flat tire. They still bumped along each day making a home for Gia and nurturing a growing love for each other, but the wheels were threatening to fall off. Father and daughter dealt with the upheaval differently. Argia, they preferred the shortened Gia, went silent and reverted to sucking her thumb, a habit Blake said she'd quit two years earlier. Blake silently deflected his emotions with single-malt scotch, tamping a simmering rage. But for how long?

Noreen squeezed his hand. "Besides, you don't drink when you have Gia on your lap, remember?"

The corners of Blake's mouth lifted. An urge to kiss him, smother his mouth with hers and absorb all his pain, washed over her right then. God, how she loved him. His biceps popped when he drew his daughter closer, protecting her from an unknown. His ex-wife was a demon all three of them still battled.

Noreen's curiosity won. "How'd it go today?"

Blake's fingers flinched ever so slightly, tightening his hold on Gia. "Remember last week I told you Lynne kept attempting physical contact and Gia resisted? She wouldn't sit on her mother's lap or hold her hand. She wouldn't even share a cookie.

"Today, Lynne *insisted* that Gia sit on her lap and that witch-doctor of a counselor supported the idea and said the intimate contact would advance Lynne's acclamation with her daughter and serve as a building block toward their reconciliation. It was pure BS. Then the counselor politely reminded me that the court orders for visitation require cooperation. Lynne smirked at that. What a coincidence that she just happened to have a copy of the judgment in front of her. I'm sure Lynne eagerly provided it. The smug look on her face said it all. She orches-trated the whole thing and there was nothing I could argue against. All the while, Lynne rocked in the rocking chair, feigning innocence."

Noreen caught her breath. "Did you make Gia do it?"

He shrugged and sipped only melted ice. "I didn't have a choice. At first, Gia flat out refused, shaking her head and covering her face with Mr. Dog and Mr. Fox." Subconsciously, Blake nudged the stuffed animals closer to his daughter. "I finally negotiated a deal with her. Ice cream every night for a week in exchange for five minutes on her mother's lap."

He squared his shoulders. "Lynne didn't make it five seconds. I swear Gia stared at me as if to signal 'watch this.' She dropped her stuffed toys in my hands, plopped on her mother's lap and started swinging her legs back and forth, rubbing her shoes against Lynne's designer pants, and bouncing as if she played in a fun house. Lynne was mortified. Her shoulders jerked and she attempted to reposition Gia's legs. But my sweet girl was having none of it. Her legs swung like a pendulum."

He chuckled at the recollection.

"Finally, Lynne snapped at Gia and said something like if you can't sit still you can't sit here and Gia was like a rocket launched off her lap and back into my arms. She refused to look at her mother again. I almost laughed in her face. But Gia was shaking like a leaf. I was so angry, I was shaking too."

"What happened then?"

"Of course, Lynne blamed me for turning Gia against her. But she was careful to conceal the rage we know she is capable of. That therapy they're forcing on her must be sinking in. Either that or she remembered the security camera in the corner.

"She didn't fly off the handle like the old Lynne. No, her accusation was more calculated, especially when she suggested that monitored visits with Gia in the future should exclude me. She wondered out loud if her visits would be more successful if only the counselor was present. Predictably, the counselor was quick to validate that notion. I tell you, the whole thing was a set up."

Noreen's heart stuttered. "Blake, you can't let that happen. Gia can't go in there alone."

"I know. I'm going to call our attorney first thing in the morning. Maybe he can figure out how to convince the judge that protecting a mother's rights in this instance will destroy the child." Gia stirred in Blake's lap, curling tighter into his embrace. "I hate to say this, Noreen, but I should've killed her when I had the chance."

Tears sprang to her eyes. "Please don't say that." She tightened her hold on his hand. "We wouldn't have been able to overcome those consequences. We'll figure out a way through this."

There was that hopeless look in his eyes again. She eased off the lounge chair and placed a soft kiss on his lips. Blake's eyes darkened with desire, sending a tingle to her thighs. They were her family now, Blake and Gia, and she'd do anything to protect them. But the only way to keep them safe was to rid their lives of Lynne Matthews.

2

Noreen surveyed the occupied hospital rooms from the nurse's horseshoe desk situated in the middle of the intensive care unit. She loved her job. The children on the pediatric surgical floor exuded hope daily, despite whatever malady landed them in a hospital bed. Most of the kids welcomed her with wide smiles, oblivious to pain and focused on what truly was important to them—the cherry Jell-O or chocolate pudding she frequently surprised them with. Blake and Gia had enlightened her about the amazing health benefits of a surprise sweet treat. She now concurred that a half-cup of ice cream worked wonders for the healing process.

She'd first encountered Argia in one of these beds, suffering from a broken wrist. That night changed her life. Rather, Blake Matthews did. Ten months ago he'd stormed onto this floor challenging her authority and demanding to see his daughter. Never in her wildest dreams would she have imagined she'd be living with the brute and loving the hell out of him and his sweet little girl. Brute hardly described the caring, sensitive, affectionate father and lover he was. She could barely stand to be apart from him, despite the joy she experienced working in this hospital.

She smiled when the elevator doors opened to reveal a flower deliveryman. Add thoughtful to that list of Blake qualities. Today marked one month that she'd returned to work full-time since the fire and the fight for her life. Blake remembered.

"Child, that man is intent on spoiling you," her co-worker Kelly chirped. She reached for the long-stem flower box. "Um, um, um, let me see what that boy is sending you now. If you weren't my best friend, I'd steal him from you."

Noreen smiled at Kelly's animated gestures, dancing in a circle with the box before setting it on the nurse station countertop, licking her fingertips and tugging on the four-inch wide black ribbon with deliberate slowness, pinkies held high. Once the ribbon untied and fell to the sides, Kelly clutched the top. "Girl, if this is a dozen roses, you're sharing half of them with me. After all, I love that man as much as you do."

Noreen's heart trilled. That wasn't possible.

Kelly's bright smile froze, and her eyebrows knitted when the lid came off. "What in Jesus' name?" She raised bulging eyes to Noreen. "Honey, this isn't from Blake."

Noreen rose and reached for the box. Three dead roses tied with a thick black cord lay in a nest of pink tissue paper. Her hand shot backward, as if touching the brown, wilted petals might scorch her fingers. She clutched her throat.

Kelly regained her wits first. She spoke as she lifted the dead flowers and rifled through the layers of tissue. "What in God's name is this? Someone's idea of a joke? I don't see a card." Now she lifted the box to scan the bottom. "What flower shop? No name printed anywhere. What the hell?"

Kelly threw the dead blooms back into the box and smashed the lid on top of it, then propped her hand on her hip. "Have you told Blake about the phone calls yet? And the flat tire last week? And now this. Noreen, this isn't good. Someone has a grudge against you and they know where you work and where you live. Girlfriend, if this doesn't make you suspicious, what will? Enough is enough."

Noreen dropped into her seat, her hand pressed against her lungs, applying pressure as if it could suppress her rapid breathing. She hadn't mentioned the nuisance calls to Blake yet. If that's what they were. He had so much else on his mind. And his job as a firefighter required focus.

As for the service call to the auto club, she'd dismissed it as an inconvenience more than anything else. The mechanic hadn't found a rupture in the tire and said it simply needed air. He suggested driving into a curb with excessive force might release a substantial amount of air and inferred perhaps she'd done just that. She hadn't argued, instead questioning her past few trips. She didn't recall striking anything, not even a speed bump in the mall parking lot. She'd downplayed the entire incident when she told Blake the next day and he hadn't seemed concerned. Of course, that was the day after a fatal fire, which hit all the men at Deep Creek Fire Station Twelve pretty hard.

She pursed her lips and regarded Kelly. "He's had so much else to worry about, I haven't bothered him about the phone calls. All of us complain about the automated calls, including you. I have no proof they are anything more than that."

"Okay, we can't prove anything about the phone calls. But these?" Kelly slapped the box. "This is a deliberate attempt to-to...I don't know what." Her hands flapped outward. "And I don't like it. Maybe we should call the police."

"And tell them what? That someone has a sick sense of humor?"

"It's one phone call. We're slow right now. Just call the police and see what they say."

"Okay, but I'm going to feel like an idiot." She retrieved her cell phone from her purse while Kelly answered another phone line. Minutes later, she disconnected the call. The sinking sensation in her stomach weighed her down. She hated feeling powerless. Kelly waited for her news.

"They won't help. I don't know who sent them and I can't tell them anything about where they came from. They wrote if off as a mean joke and told me to do the same. I'm on my own to figure it out."

The elevator door slid open again and they turned to watch Paramedic Joe Lystle stroll toward them.

Seeing the flower box, he grinned. "Bet I know who those are from."

She'd prefer Joe didn't see its contents, but Kelly had other ideas. "Not Blake, no way." She lifted the lid. "This is from some sick ass person out there and we all better start paying attention to who has Noreen in their crosshairs."

Noreen slammed the lid closed. "Kelly, please. It's not a big deal." But it was and Joe's widened eyes and slack jaw indicated he realized it too.

"Christ, Noreen, did these just come? Who delivered them?" He scanned the halls in every direction, as if the delivery person might still be lingering in one of the corridors. He wasn't.

"Is there a card?" She might as well have not been there since Kelly answered each of his queries.

"Did you tell Blake?"

"No, she didn't and if she doesn't, that boy is gettin' a phone call from me. There's too many coincidences going on for them to be a coincidence. Do you hear what I'm saying?"

The radio on his belt pinged. "Rob's waiting for me in the ambulance. I gotta go. I just stopped to tell you Brittni will pick up Gia after school but she's taking her to our place instead of your home. We're waiting for the cable company to make a service call. The storm last night damaged our connection. Their arrival window is between three and six. Once they leave,

Brittni will take Gia to Blake's and I'm off at six so I'll be there tonight too. I'll see you tomorrow morning when you get home from work. We can talk about this then if you want."

Noreen called to him as he stepped on the elevator. "Joe don't mention this to Blake, please. I'll tell him, I promise."

He nodded and the doors closed.

Kelly leveled a mean glare at her.

"I'll tell him tomorrow as soon as he gets home. I swear." Tell him what, she wasn't sure. That someone was trying to spook her? That she had the crazy feeling it was his ex-wife? Then how crazy would that make him?

3

Blake slammed his cell phone down on the desk, grateful that the tapping on his office door provided an excuse to hang up on his attorney. Well, more like abruptly end the call by barking "find a way, dammit" so that the man understood he wasn't happy.

"Come," he called to his visitor. "Hey, Joe, what's going on?"

"I only need a minute. Is this a bad time, Lewey?"

Blake smiled at the affectionate abbreviation of his rank as lieutenant and ran his fingers through his hair. "Nah, come in. Lately there haven't been many good times. How can I help you?"

Joe leaned on the back of one of two chairs that faced his desk. "It's nothing I need. Brittni will be late taking Gia home to your place because we have a cable service call lined up. I want to make sure you know. I stopped at the hospital on our last run and told Noreen. And also, when I clock out at six, I'll be with her and Gia for the night if you're okay with that."

A slow blush crossed his cheeks. "I'll sleep on the couch, though, not with Brittni. Not in front of Gia."

Blake smiled at the way Joe dropped his gaze, like a

schoolboy caught mooning over the girl in the desk in front of him. Joe said he was off at six. Usually, their shifts coincided—twenty-four on and forty-eight off. "How'd we get on different schedules this month?"

Joe nodded. "I switched with Raymundo so he could take a two-week honeymoon. Remember?"

Right. That wedding had been much needed fun for all three of them. He, Noreen, and Gia dancing together, laughing, not even thinking about the gloomy shadow Lynne's intrusion into their lives cast. Gia had really blossomed over the last ten months, always giggling at something, asking more questions than he could answer, and filling his heart to overflow. It didn't seem possible that he could love his daughter more than he already did but each day, she took ownership of another piece. He credited Noreen with shining light into both their lives with the love she drenched them in. Ironic, since she and Gia still feared the dark. But he'd never been so happy. Until his ex-wife's progress back into society blanketed them like a black cloud. The glow around all three of them had dimmed.

The arrangement he negotiated with Joe's girlfriend, Brittni, worked well for all of them. When he worked his twenty-four-hour shift and Noreen staffed the hospital for her seven-to-seven-night shift, he paid Brittni to care for Gia, staying in his home in the guest room overnight. Brittni had a degree in early childhood development and was working toward becoming a full-time nanny. She was the only one he trusted with his daughter, besides his mother.

Gia rarely let strangers close, but Brittni and Joe had earned her confidence. Joe had been the first to scoop up Gia after her escape from the cellar her mother had locked her in last year. Finding his daughter was a debt owed to Joe that he'd never fully repay. It had been Joe's idea to keep the house under constant surveillance, and he'd logged the most hours there.

"Once Raymundo returns, I believe our schedules are

synced again. If you're concerned with my staying with Brittni, just say so, Lewey. I can stay at our place."

His hand passed through the air. "It's not a concern at all. Make yourself at home while you're there. The liquor cabinet is stocked. And you don't have to sleep on the couch. Noreen and I share a bed. Gia understands that when two people love each other, it's what they do. Don't be surprised if she crawls in with you though. She's been doing that more and more lately."

Especially following a forced visit with her mother. His poor baby girl had nightmares after spending time with The Captain, his ex-wife's self-proclaimed status in their marriage. Lynne Matthews liked to believe she called all the shots. Maybe she did. Even while still in supervised custody for reduced charges from attempted murder and suspicion of arson she was making his life a living hell.

Joe blushed again. "I'll see. Maybe I'll sleep on the couch anyway. With some of the stuff that's been happening, I feel better about being at the house with them. I won't sleep as soundly on the sofa."

Blake's stomach cinched. "What stuff? Something going on between you and Brittni? You two are ideal for each other."

Joe straightened and cleared his throat. "Ah, no. We're good. I'm sure Noreen will catch you up on, uh, the latest." He backed toward the door. "You know me, always trying to fix things."

A premonition of evil straightened Blake's spine. "Joey? You're trying real hard not to tell me something. What is it?"

"Nothing, Sir. Nothing that I know for certain." His hand grabbed the doorknob. "I'll close this behind me. See you later, Lewey."

Blake stared at the blank door. Now what did he have to deal with? His mind was already spinning after the conversation with his attorney. He planned to challenge Lynne's attempt to spend time with Gia without Blake overseeing each visit, but the attorney wasn't optimistic in lieu of the court's favoritism toward the mother's rights. The purpose of the visits was to rebuild the relationship between mother and daughter and if the judge interpreted Blake's presence as an obstacle to that goal, he'd likely ban Blake from the room. As if one hour once a week in a strange house could erase the memory of her mother breaking her arm or locking her in a dungeon or frightening the hell out of her. He doubted Gia would ever trust her mother again. He certainly wouldn't.

His attorney's phone call left a sour taste in his mouth and Joey's comments added to his feeling that evil lurked just around the bend.

Noreen couldn't take phone calls while at work, but he texted her anyway. *Stay safe. I love you.*

Where Noreen was concerned, he needed to do a better job at both.

4

Noreen sank deeper into the Jacuzzi tub and chuckled at the growing mountain of bubbles the pulsating jets created. If only life could be as carefree and light as their foamy weightlessness.

This bath had been on the fringes of her mind all day, as well as the glass of wine that accompanied the long soak. The hot water relieved the tension in her neck and relaxed the ever-present tightness around the damaged skin on her back and shoulders. Blake said the scars were barely noticeable but to her observation, they stood out like an early red tulip buried in a blanket of spring snow. Blake and Gia saw her through the eyes of love and didn't see what she saw.

That image warmed her more than the bath—that they had both fallen in love with her. And hearing Blake's voice turned up the heat.

"Yoo-hoo! Are any of the women I love around?" His footsteps fell on the hardwood stairs as he climbed to the second floor. He'd been to the City Building for a monthly administrators' meeting, promising to be home for dinner.

"In here." She eyed the extra glass and the wine chilling in the cooling decanter. So far, the evening was progressing as planned.

Blake's ear-to-ear grin shot straight to her core. "Well, you sure know how to make a man happy to be home." He leaned over the tub to touch his lips to hers and didn't resist when her soapy hand pressed into his hair to deepen the kiss. That familiar look darkened his eyes, the one he revealed after they made love.

"Where's Gia?" He whispered the question while his fingers outlined her jaw and traveled slowly down her throat. His touch set her on fire. Good thing she was immersed in water.

"She's with your mom for the night. Movie night at Grammy's. Doesn't it sound wonderful?"

Blake's fingers dipped below the water to caress her breast. "I'll say." He found her nipple and rotated it smoothly between his fingers. "How long do you plan to be in this tub?" He leaned in for a second kiss and she allowed him to explore her mouth with his tongue.

"You taste delicious, by the way. This might be my favorite wine, whatever it is." His gaze danced along the water surface.

Noreen lifted her dripping hand and reached for the top button on his shirt. "Glad to hear. Why don't you pour yourself a glass and join me?"

His eyebrows hiked to his hairline. "Join you?"

She'd undone three buttons. "Don't tell me you're too old for a bubble bath. I'll make it worth your while." She'd reached his belt buckle and felt the stretched fabric of his trousers. "It appears part of you likes the idea." When she rolled her hand along the bulge in his pants, he gulped.

He cupped her breast and kissed her hard enough to take her breath away. But that was her usual reaction to this man whom she needed as much as she needed air to breathe. Almost a year ago, they shared their first kiss when she'd arrived home from work in the morning and he barged into her apartment minutes later. That kiss had landed them in each other's arms and in her bed. Since that encounter, their passion intensified any time they touched each other.

Blake leaned backward and straightened, removing his shirt and white cotton T-shirt as he stood. He reached for the wine bottle, poured his and topped off hers. "No ma'am, I'm not too old for a bath. But be warned, I'll take up a lot of room in there. You might be squished in all those bubbles." He lowered his zipper.

Watching him undress was delicious torture. She licked her lips when he dropped his pants and his desire sprang to attention. Like her, he recognized her craving and smiled, reaching to take a long swig from his glass.

Noreen sat up and her breasts emerged from the water, immediately drawing his interest. "I've considered the space limitations of this tub, sir." She grinned and lowered her eyelids seductively. "With you in here, I'll have to sit on your lap."

NINETY MINUTES LATER, their fingertips and toes wrinkled from the water and their appetites for each other sated, they cuddled on a loveseat on the back deck and munched on a pepperoni pizza. Fireflies dotted the night sky as if floating on the soft piano music playing through the sound system.

Blake sighed. "You are a healer on many levels, you know that?"

His bare foot was propped on the wicker table in front of them and Noreen ran her toes across it. "Thank you. It's easy to nurture someone you love."

His muscles flexed when he drew her closer. "I'm a lucky man." He kissed her temple. "I had an interesting chat with Joey yesterday. I had the feeling he thought I should know something but didn't want to be the one to tell me. Something pertaining to you. Any idea what that was about?"

She sat up and placed her wine glass on the table. She laced her fingers in his hand. "Some weird incidents have Joe and Kelly on edge. Maybe me too."

Blake's fingers tightened but he didn't press for more information. He waited, letting her explain at her own pace.

She shrugged. "Some hang up phone calls. Well, I can't even call them hang ups because whoever it is, they stay on the line. They don't bother to hang up. They might simply be robocalls." Her shoulders drooped. "Honestly, I don't know."

Blakes eyebrows knitted. "Robocalls are an automated voice that speaks. They don't keep the line open. How many calls?"

She shrugged again, tilting her head to the right. "I don't answer all the time. I don't know how many. Enough to seem odd. At first, maybe one every other day. Now, maybe one or two a day. It must depend on my schedule. I only get them when I'm here at home."

Blake dropped his foot to the floor and sat up. "Do you hear what you're saying? Someone knows your schedule and calls when you aren't at the hospital. Where am I? Was I here?"

She shook her head.

"Only calls when I'm not here? Sweetheart, do you know what this sounds like?"

She nodded. "Yes, yes I do. It sounds like stalking. It definitely seems orchestrated. But our schedules are posted at the hospital. It's not a secret when I'm working or off."

Blake arched one skeptical eyebrow. "You think someone from work is harassing you? Why? Have you reprimanded anyone? Given them a reason to taunt you?"

She hadn't. And she doubted very much it was a colleague. "No. I can't explain it, Blake, so I don't know what I think. Um, there's something else."

He sat up straighter.

"I received a box of dead roses. They came right to the ICU floor but I didn't pay enough attention to the deliveryman. I was excited because I thought they were from you. Joe saw them. That's probably what made him mention something without really telling you."

Blake's chest rose with his intake of breath. "Was there a card or any—"

"No, we couldn't find any clue about the sender. Nothing on the box. And like I said, I didn't observe anything about the deliveryman except that he was a man. I've never seen him before."

"You were planning to tell me all this, weren't you?"

"Of course. I hoped maybe I could figure it out first, but we both know what we think. And who we suspect. I'm afraid to add to the drama she's already created, especially since we have no way to be sure."

"I'm pretty sure Lynne is behind it, sweetheart. Don't ask me how she's managing it. But the tactics are her trademark. Backstabbing and sinister. Anything else? Have you told me everything?"

"Yes. Kelly thinks the flat tire is connected and, possibly yes, it could be. Blake, we can't overreact to any of this. That would play right into her hands." She nudged her way under his arm and pressed him back into the loveseat, allowing them to resume their embrace. He placed a light kiss on her forehead.

"I'm not overreacting. I'd like to know what her game is. She should have learned her lesson last time. Going after you or Gia is a big mistake. I won't let it happen again."

"Neither will I. She'll never catch me off guard again like she did when she shoved me down those cellar stairs." The memory of that fall caused the leg she'd broken to pulse and she stretched it to the table. "She's trying to throw you off balance so she can make a case before the judge that you are irrational. She's trying to get a rise out of you any way she can."

He laughed. "Believe me, sweetheart, she could be the last woman on earth and she couldn't get a rise from me." His open-mouthed kiss left her breathless. "That's your department and you are damn good at it."

He stared into her eyes. "Promise you'll tell me about anything else unusual that happens, no matter how small. And right away, not after Kelly and Joe and the world knows before I do."

She smiled. "I promise. And you promise you won't do anything without discussing it with me first. Promise me you won't lose your temper if anything else happens."

He thought about it so long, she wondered if he'd answer. Finally, he agreed.

"May I ask one more thing?" She nuzzled his neck, knowing she wasn't playing fair. He was a sucker for neck kisses. She interpreted his soft groan as consent. She sat up to look at him directly.

"Will you cut back on the scotch, please? I'd hate for us to have to think clearly on a night when you've had as many as you sometimes have and can't be logical."

He turned his head away and exhaled. But he didn't argue. That was a good sign, wasn't it? She didn't want to ruin their romantic night. "Let's not spoil tonight by talking about this now, okay? Our life together has been wonderful. I've never been happier. Lynne's reappearance will just be a blip on the radar screen if we handle it correctly. We'll figure it out and then live happily ever after, just like in Gia's fairy princess books."

At the mention of her name, he relaxed. Gia was the reason Blake lived. Noreen felt the tension release from his shoulders. The corners of his mouth lifted. "She never tires of having those books read to her. And even though she knows the endings, she's still excited every time. It amazes me."

He drew her tighter into his arms and kissed the top of her

shoulder. "You amaze me too. We're not finished discussing this but you're right, it can wait. I miss that little minx but I'm happy to have you all to myself."

He kissed her deeply, and the tingle seeped all the way to her toes. Dead roses and creepy phone calls didn't matter. This man's love for her was what was important. She returned his kiss, equaling the intensity.

He traced her jawline with his fingertip and stared into her eyes. "You're really something, you know that? I'm not sure you knew what you were getting into when you opened your apartment door for me. Not where Gia is concerned. She's as bright and full of promise as a new day. But me—I come with a lot of baggage. You've already had to fight this ugly monster from my past and now, like a cancer coming out of remission, she's coming back for round two. You didn't sign on for that."

She flexed her bicep. "I'm good for ten rounds, buddy. Don't worry about me."

Blake chuckled. "It's not your fight."

She wasn't going to allow a conversation about his ex wreck her plans for this night. She'd almost died protecting this man's daughter and she'd do it again to save him or Gia. But she'd rather love him to death. "Sorry, Mr. Matthews, but it is. You and Gia are my family now. I can't even express the depth of my love for the two of you." She stood and straddled him, easing onto his lap facing him.

Blake's eyebrows rose in surprise.

"Let me show you instead." She covered his mouth with hers before he could respond.

5

When Noreen arrived home from work two days later, Blake was leaning against the kitchen counter, sipping his coffee. It never mattered how tired she was or how intense her shift might have been, seeing him lightened every concern she might have. Her heart fluttered as she waltzed into his arms for a sweet kiss.

"Good morning. Did you get Gia to school okay?" she asked.

He nodded and canted his head toward the kitchen table. A vase with a dozen red roses sat in the center. Noreen gasped.

"What are those for?"

"I asked Joey to stop over for a beer last night so we could talk about the rose delivery and toss some theories around. I'm sorry I forgot last Tuesday was an anniversary of sorts."

"Oh, Blake. It wasn't that big a deal, honest."

He poured her a cup of coffee and reached in the fridge for the cream. "I should've remembered it. Gia overheard us talking and I admitted that I screwed up.' He chuckled. "She literally stomped her little foot and reprimanded me. Brittni helped her make the card." Noreen reached for the folded piece of pink paper and smiled at the lopsided red heart drawn on the front.

Inside, helter-skelter block letters scrawled across the page. "Daddy is sorry. I love you. Gia Matthews."

Blake read over her shoulder, laughed, and wrapped his arms around her waist. "I swear I'm losing ground with my own daughter because of you. And my crew, too. Joey is ready to start his twenty-four-hour surveillance again on Lynne to protect you. That man used to be loyal to me. Now I think he and my whole damn squad would go to the wall for you. We've all fallen in love with you."

She didn't need hot coffee to heat up. Blake's words did a fine job. "Robin's band of merry men were enamored with Maid Marian too. It didn't make him less of a leader."

He kissed the back of her neck. "You're a remarkable woman, d'you know that? You make me weak and strong, all at the same time. But I'm worried about you and what's been going on."

She turned in his arms. "Please tell me you're not going to allow your men to take turns staking out Lynne. If she discovered that, it would be ammunition for the judge. We'd lose Gia."

"It wasn't my idea last time. Joe was convinced Lynne was behind your disappearance and he organized the round-the-clock watch on Lynne. Thank God he did or we might not have found you and Gia locked in that basement. He's equally suspicious now and I agree with him."

She stepped out of his embrace and walked to the sink. "Well, stalking Lynne because we think she's stalking me isn't the answer."

"You're right and that isn't the plan. There is no real plan except to caution you to always be aware of your surroundings and on your guard." He raised his hand to interrupt her response. "I know, I know, you already do that. But can we discuss this dead flower delivery a little more? Joey said by the time he walked back outside, the delivery van was gone. He circled the block but didn't find it. We agree, that was a long shot. So that brings it back to you."

Her chest tightened. She stupidly hadn't paid attention. "I told you everything."

"You said a man delivered them. Can you describe him?"

"I hardly noticed him. When he stepped off the elevator with the long-stem box I was excited to think you'd sent me flowers. My focus was on the box, not him."

"Did he ask for you by name?"

She rubbed the back of her neck and stared at the ceiling, walking her mind back in time. "No, he didn't ask who I was or if I was Noreen Jensen. I was sitting at the horseshoe and, on the lanyard, my badge falls below the desk. He couldn't have seen my identity. There wasn't a delivery label on the box with my name on it either. He must have known who I was and that they were for me."

"But how did he know you were you? What'd he look like? Tall? Short? White? Black? Blond? You noticed something about him, you had to. Beer belly? Gym rat? What about his voice? Did he say anything?"

A lump rose in her throat. "He said, 'Enjoy your flowers, Miss Jensen.'" Her stomach turned, rebelling against the coffee she'd just swallowed.

"How'd he *know* it was you? Was Kelly at the desk too?"

"I-I don't know. No, she was just approaching the horseshoe."

"Did she see him? Can she give me a description?"

Her hand began to shake and she set her coffee cup down next to Blake's. What would it take to move this entire incident behind her? "I-I'm not sure. She was excited like me and going on and on about how you spoil me. I don't think either one of us paid any attention to the courier."

"Joey said he didn't see him either."

She closed her eyes to relive the moment one more time. The elevator bell sounded. The doors slid open. He smiled as he approached the horseshoe. Dammit. Her gaze had been on the box. She nodded when he spoke, but she barely looked up. The elevator door opened again immediately after he touched the button. And he disappeared.

"No, the man was gone before Joe stepped out of the elevator. He arrived at least five minutes after the delivery. He saw the box and grinned, thinking you'd sent me flowers too. That's what we all thought. But once Kelly showed him the contents and blabbed about the flat tire and phone calls, he grew concerned."

"And rightly so. Tell me again about the phone calls."

She shrugged. "I honestly didn't think they were anything, Blake. Not really. I mean they creeped me out, but I just wrote them off as nuisance calls."

"You said sometimes you answered them. What did you hear?"

Her eyes jammed shut. "Nothing. Whoever was on the other end never said anything."

"So you could hear someone?"

She leveled her gaze on his gray eyes. This much she was certain of. "No, but I could tell the line was open. Not silence, but a vibe."

Blake grew quiet, staring at the floor. He rubbed small circles on her back, a gesture he often made while holding Gia. "You said there isn't a co-worker mad at you. You haven't mentioned any patients you've lost, or any irate parents in sweaty ball uniforms."

They still joked about their first meeting, when Blake rushed from the softball field to the hospital and tried to bully her to gain access to Argia. It hadn't worked.

"I've asked myself that same question and there is only one

answer. One person. But it's impossible. She's been under doctor's care and for the last few weeks, under twenty-four-hour supervision in Dalton House. It can't be Lynne."

Blake's head snapped up. "That doesn't mean she isn't behind all this. I'll never believe she is mentally balanced. Or that she's forgiven me for divorcing her and taking Gia from her, no matter what she states under oath. Or what some quack of a doctor certifies. She's still a scheming, manipulative woman scorned."

"But how could Lynne manage something like this if she is constantly monitored?" She counted off her points on her fingers. "She couldn't have been in the parking lot to tamper with my tire because she was confined to the house. She doesn't have a phone to make phone calls or to order dead flowers, for that matter. And she has no income, does she? How could it be Lynne?"

Blake stared at her. "How can it not be?"

6

Lynne Matthews slipped into her designer heels and tugged on the bolero jacket of her pantsuit. If only she had her six-drawer cherry wood jewelry armoire to accessorize with. But her jewelry wasn't safe in this house with the derelicts she begrudgingly called her housemates. *She barely felt safe.*

Dalton House was no place for a woman of her status, cramped in a two-story hellhole inhabited by reformed drug addicts, thieves and petty criminals. She hadn't committed real crimes like them and besides, she suffered from diminished mental capacity. She hadn't meant to hurt that whore-nurse that her husband was sleeping with. Nor would she ever harm a hair on her beautiful daughter's head. She'd simply been under so much stress, what with Blake divorcing her, seeking full custody of Argia, forcing her to move out of their home. Pressuring her. Threatening her. She hadn't been able to handle it all so she wasn't responsible for her actions, not really. And the fire? Well, that was simply an accident. None of it had been premeditated. Everyone knew what a devoted wife and mother she was. Neighbors had attested to it. And the authorities bought it hook, line and sinker.

Today, obediently under a physician's care and with prescribed medicines she cleverly managed not to take, she was fine. She'd played that hand like a Vegas high-stakes gambler—the bewildered, disoriented, mother appalled when finally confronted with her alleged conduct. No way would she ever harm her daughter. Argia was her life. She must have been out of her mind, unaware of her actions, misguided by her body's hormonal imbalance. Yes, yes, psychiatric treatment and meds were acceptable. Anything to restore her relationship with her sweet little girl.

Her lips edged up into a smirk. She'd easily won that game. Six months in that psychiatric hospital was better than jail. After all, she didn't have a prior criminal history. The food in that place had been horrendous but she'd lost weight so that was an upside.

And then sixty-days in this halfway house to acclimate her back into society. Not that these wretches were her social peers. But she had to follow their playbook if she wanted released from their 24/7 monitoring. Yielding to their silly rules had placated everyone so far. She could endure a little longer.

Today's shopping expedition with Dalton House's chief of medical staff along with her parole officer observing her interaction with the real world was designed to determine if her mind was clear, and she could process and make informed, intelligent decisions. For them, it was a demonstration of her acceptance of societal norms. For her, it was an encore performance and she had the lead role. This would be a piece of cake.

She squared her shoulders and forced a smile when the door to her room opened. That was one of the things she detested about Fran, her assigned life coach. The woman had no regard for privacy. She never knocked. And there were no locks on these damn doors.

"My, my Lynne, you look stunning. A little overdressed for the grocery store, perhaps, but it suits you."

Lynne feigned embarrassment and smoothed the front of her jacket. "Oh, Fran, should I change? I do so want to make a good impression on my parole officer and the doctor. It's the first time they'll see me outside of this house. And quite frankly, it's been so long since I've been able to wear my nicer things, I couldn't help myself."

Fran clucked like a chicken. "It will have to do. There's no time to change. Come, come. Follow me."

Like a school child obeying the teacher, Lynne picked up the fanny pack included in her Resident's Welcome Basket and followed Fran out the door. Keeping her designer bags here wasn't safe either but she'd be damned if she'd strap on this hideous daypack like the other women. It dangled from her thumb and fingers as if it were contaminated.

"Now remember," Fran lectured over her shoulder, "this is an exercise designed to demonstrate your socialization skills and your comprehension of healthy life choices. We'll be observing your interfacing with others but it's also a test of your independence, so I won't be at your elbow."

Thank God. "I'll try my best not to disappoint you." The words almost caught in her throat. This excursion called for subdued mollification, not the rage that simmered just below her skin. So be it. Her lungs filled with a determined breath. Today, The Captain would be the epitome of submission. Whatever the experts suggested, she'd agree to. It was only a matter of time before they released her but it damn well better happen soon.

She had a plan for her life after rehab, one that included payback. Today's adventure would advance that too, as long as Phillip remembered to show up.

Lynne studied her list while Fran drove to the grocery store. She'd memorized the combinations of meals served nightly and could easily duplicate the disgusting dishes. Ground meat for meatloaf and hamburgers, canned tomato sauce and pasta noodles. Spaghetti was the cook's favorite, probably because it served so many with very little effort. Bags of apples, oranges, and potatoes. Potatoes cooked every imaginable way and in some she'd never imagine. She might never eat a potato in any form again. She'd certainly never permit Argia to have them.

At least the produce aisle and salad greens would give her palate some satisfaction. Plus, that's where Phillip was supposed to meet her. They should be able to confer while waiting for the vegetable misters to stop spraying.

Dalton House rules forbade any contact with friends or family outside of the supervised visits at the halfway house. Phone calls with her public defender were monitored and any mail was scanned and read before delivery. That didn't matter. She received no mail.

Phillip promised to disguise himself today. Her parole officer had never met him, but that busybody Fran might recognize him from his visits. It'd better be a good disguise. It would be nice to see him again. Even better to sleep with him. Not as good as making love with Blake. But that would come soon enough.

PHILLIP TOOK one last toke of his joint when he saw Lynne step out of the mini van. He'd imagined she might have to wear an orange prison jumpsuit, seeing as how she was a criminal out among real folk. She looked pretty hot in that dark pantsuit and those spiked heels that could bring his dick to attention in two point seven seconds. She never wore those shoes when he visited Dalton House. Always some sloppy prison-issued slippers. *Rehabilitation*, his brain corrected, having heard Lynne say it a million times. She was locked up, for gawd's sake. Dalton House was a carpeted jail.

He squinted through the lingering smoke. That hag Fran was with her. She felt sorry for Lynne so, like everyone in her line of sight, Lynne used her. She'd even conned the hag out of some bucks. How much money could the woman have? She worked for the government in a nothing job. Lynne hadn't said how much Fran gave her or how she finagled the money out of her. She called it a loan, but he knew better. Lynne was a master at manipulating people, including him. He doubted that Lynne wrapped those long legs around Fran's hips when she asked for favors. Damn, he missed fucking her.

He flicked the ash off his doobie onto the floor mat. No sense wasting it. After this little performance, he planned to get as high as the birds. He smoothed the mustache with his thumb and forefinger. The damn thing stuck to his lip and smelled funky. He kinda liked how he looked though. Like a gangster from an old movie. He shoulda thought about a fedora.

The disguise better make her happy because he didn't exactly have good news for her. She expected him to rent an apartment but hell, he wasn't made of money. Lately, it seemed all the extra dough he made he gave to her. How could someone need so many things in jail? *Rehabilitation.*

At least he found a place. Not an upscale neighborhood like she insisted. Not even a decent apartment building, to be honest. But his buddy was a clean freak, so the place looked respectable. The smoke smell would go away once the windows were opened. She was under the gun to have a place to live and get a job. He couldn't wait to see how she managed that. If she had any skills beyond sex, he hadn't witnessed them.

She said the apartment was supposed to be temporary so what did it matter where it was? She was cooking up some big plans. Something to put them on easy street, she promised. A chuckle rumbled through his chest. He already lived on easy street.

Lynne followed behind Fran to the store entrance. Sashayed better described that walk of hers. Geez. He needed laid.

SHE SPOTTED Phillip in front of the lettuce, a carry basket hanging on his arm, his ball cap tugged low and his sunglasses riding the brim. He hadn't shaved for several days and pasted a fake dark mustache above his lip. Beards didn't do it for her but oddly, this was a turn-on. Perhaps because he'd done it for her. The dark shadow on his face contrasted to his clean white T-shirt over blue jeans. Usually, Phillip visited in a coat and tie, the only one he owned. He'd bought it at a resale shop. She cringed at the thought of wearing someone else's clothes and refused to touch him when he visited. But Phillip hadn't seemed to mind the hand-me-down.

Dressing down like this transformed him from the suit-wearing boyfriend to a casual shopper. She breathed a sigh of relief. It was a suitable camouflage.

She guided her grocery cart alongside him and bent over it as if to rearrange the items inside. The movement allowed her silk top to fall and offered Phillip a sweet view of her breasts.

A smile exploded across his face. The man was a chump when it came to sex.

"I can't wait to get my hands on you," he growled.

Lynne straightened and smiled. "Tell me we're one step closer." She turned toward the array of leafy products and waited for the sprayers to shut off.

"I got us a place. It's my buddy's but he snagged a drilling job in South Carolina and is gone for at least six months. So the place is ours. Rent-free to boot."

"But what name did you use? They could check the lease."

Phillip winked at her. "No sweat. I have a fake ID to match it."

"Two bedrooms, right? Argia must have her own room."

He nodded and reached for a bundle of red lettuce, inspecting it as if he might purchase it. Fat chance he'd add something healthy to the chips, queso dip, and cooked chicken wings already in his basket.

"It's small but yeah, two bedrooms. He uses it as a junk room. We can move everything to his storage spot. Every tenant has one."

"You told him I want to paint and decorate, didn't you?"

Based on Phillip's shrug, he hadn't. She didn't really care.

"I should be released soon. I'll be permitted to call you to pick me up. Are you still using a burner phone? I don't know the number."

"Signal like always, Babe. I'll come."

Just like a well-trained dog. "Phillip?" His head pivoted. "I can't wait for your hands on me either."

Tossing two dripping bundles of lettuce in her cart, she rolled it away. They'd devised the simplest of means to communicate. Something Lynne watched in a movie but couldn't recall the title. Whenever she wanted Phillip to visit, she placed a potted plant in her window. He drove by the transitional living home daily on his way to his favorite bar, a place she went to once with him and would never return. For God's sake, her wedges stuck to the floor.

Phillip had a photography degree he did nothing with. When they first met, his ambition was to make porn films. He wasn't motivated to pursue even that bizarre goal. He wasn't motivated to do much of anything except drink and get high and think about sex. But he suited her purposes.

He never missed her signal to visit and the next day, he'd appear. Sports coat and tie and dirt caked under his nails.

When she asked, he deposited money in her commissary

account although she had no idea how he earned it and didn't want to know. As dull as he was, some days he was her only ray of hope that she'd return to the real world. He couldn't comprehend her dissatisfaction with failure and loose ends. His solution was to shrug his shoulders and blow it off. He'd blow an O-ring of smoke and say, "Fuck it. It is what it was," not only speaking in redundancies but quoting the phrase incorrectly. The perfect example of failure.

But she had a problem and he was her solution to the dilemma with Noreen Jensen. She was both a loose end and a failed mission.

7

Noreen cherished these nights when Blake worked, and it was just her and Gia. It wasn't that she competed with Blake for the child's attention because Gia's love for both of them seemed boundless. But Blake was always her first choice for a cuddle or a kiss or a surprise hide-and-seek game. Noreen understood the magnetism. Blake was her first choice for just about everything.

Still, the girl-time together strengthened a bond that was born when they clung to each other in that black hole in the cellar of Blake's old house. Plus, Argia seemed starved for 'mother time' and Noreen was happy to provide it. Tonight, they planned to polish each other's nails and watch a movie. Gia clapped and jumped up and down when the two of them purchased the neon pink at the discount store days earlier. For a six-year-old, Argia's hand was rather steady and her artistic abilities above average. Noreen wasn't concerned that her fingers would look dipped in color. She'd have to remove it before her next shift at the hospital anyway.

Argia had just finished applying polish to Noreen's pinkie and ring finger on her left hand when the lights went out.

Noreen momentarily froze, then tapped the flashlight app on her cell phone laying at her elbow and held it up to shine throughout the room. This felt eerily familiar.

"How come the lights went out, Weenie?" Gia already had gotten out of her chair and moved to stand beside her at the kitchen table. "I don't like the dark."

No, ever since she'd been locked in that cavern by her mother, Argia required lots of lights on in the house. Usually in every room. She slept with the lamp on beside her bed.

Noreen relaxed with the lights on too. She wrapped her arms around Gia's waist and drew her closer. "It's probably just a power outage. Maybe there's a storm coming." But no thunder had rolled across the sky and the six o'clock weatherman hadn't predicted rain.

"We have plenty of candles and real flashlights, honey. Don't worry." She stood and took Gia's hand. "Let's find them now."

The candles were closest and in minutes, Noreen had three lit and spaced out across the kitchen counter. Argia clung to her pant leg the whole time she completed the task.

"Your daddy has a bin of flashlights on the first shelf in the garage. We'll take a couple of those and make it light as day."

Noreen had insisted on flashlights strategically placed throughout the house. Practically every room had one. Blake hadn't argued with her request, understanding that being locked in the dark for days and fighting for your life was traumatizing. Besides, having a flashlight in her hand might have saved her life that night in the hospital when Lynne attacked her.

She and Gia had talked to therapists but all the counseling in the world couldn't erase their mutual fear of the dark. Right now, seeing the shadows cast by the flickering light, her heart raced.

She switched on the mini red pocket light that stayed in the silverware drawer, slipped the wrist strap over Gia's hand, and closed her fingers around it.

"Weenie?"

"It's okay, honey. We'll get more lights. You just hold onto this one until we do." She'd whispered similar words to the child when their lives depended on it and Gia clung to the light even after the battery died.

Her lungs caught the air. "We're safe here. Don't be afraid. I bet every house in the neighborhood is in the dark right now. It happens sometimes. We'll get more flashlights and then look out the windows. Hang onto me."

"I want Mr. Dog and Mr. Fox."

Of course. The four of them had walked—make that crawled—through hell and come out alive. Noreen guided them to the kitchen table and Argia crushed the stuffed animals to her chest. The pocket light swung from Gia's arm, its slim beam bouncing wildly off the floor and the baseboards.

Reaching to take her hand again, Noreen moved toward the garage. Gia's grip was sweaty and vise-like. Together they shined lights into the pitch-black garage. The plastic container was easily reachable. Noreen switched on the first flashlight her hand touched and the beam filled their corner of the garage. "Here ya go, sweetie. Hold this one instead." Gia wrapped both hands around it.

Noreen retrieved a second flashlight and, once it shined brightly, she snapped off her phone and dropped it into her jeans pocket. Since her abduction, the phone was never out of reach.

She removed two more lights, flicking them on as well, and held the trio like a bridal bouquet. Argia stared up at her wide-eyed.

"Let's go look out the front door. Maybe some of the neighbors will come outside and we can turn this into a light beam party." God how she hoped all of the houses on the street were dark. If they weren't, being outside might still be safer. If she screamed, someone was bound to hear.

Argia gripped her pant leg and followed her down the hall toward the entrance. Halfway toward their destination, her cell phone rang in her pocket, slicing the shadowed stillness like a razor blade. Her heart catapulted to her throat and Gia screamed a cry of terror. She dropped to her knees and embraced Argia. "It's just my phone, honey. Nothing to be afraid of." The falter in her voice wasn't reassuring. Seeing it was Blake calling, she smiled, and immediately relaxed. "It's your daddy, Gia, calling to check on us."

"How're my two favorite girls?" Blake's deep voice flowed into her ear, down her neck, and through her whole being, enfolding her in a blanket of security. Even so, her response sounded weak. "Extremely glad to hear your voice. I'm putting you on speaker so Gia can hear. What's going on?"

"A utility truck took out a main transformer on the West End. Power is out for the whole grid. A couple thousand homes is the preliminary estimate, including our station. We're running on back-up generators. Are you two okay?"

"Daddy, I want the lights back on. Turn them on, please."

"Aw Peanut, if I could turn them on for you, I would. But this is bigger than Daddy can handle."

"I don't like it, Daddy. Can you come home?" Her bottom lip quivered and tears filled her eyes. Noreen tightened her hug.

"Not just yet, Peanut. I'll be home as soon as I can but, in the meantime, I need you to be brave and to comfort Noreen. You know she doesn't like the dark. Can you do that for me?"

But panic already seized the child. Her breath came in rapid bursts, tears rolled down her cheeks and she started to shake uncontrollably.

"I don't like the dark either, Daddy. Come home."

Noreen raised the phone to her ear. "I need to hang up before this blows out of control. I'll call you back." She didn't wait for Blake to say goodbye. She disconnected the call, rolled backward into a sitting position, and dragged Argia onto her lap. "Relax, honey, we're fine. We're safe in our home."

The doorbell rang and Noreen gasped. Argia wet herself.

"Noreen?" Carole Matthews knocked and called from the front porch. "Noreen? It's Carole. Are you home?"

She didn't want to let go of Gia, afraid to stop rocking her or relax her grip. She yelled to Blake's mother's shadow through the beveled glass. "We're here, Carole. Can you let yourself in?"

The key turned in the lock and the door swung open. Noreen aimed one of the flashlights along the floor, lighting a path to their position. "We're right here. We just talked to Blake. The power is out there too."

Carole didn't need an explanation as to why the two of them sat on the hallway floor and Noreen continually rocked her granddaughter. She dropped down beside them and wrapped her arm around Noreen's shoulders. Argia's face was buried in Noreen's chest and her grandmother gently caressed the back of her head.

"It's all right, my darling, Grammy is here to take care of both of you."

Noreen's heart jerked and tears welled in her eyes. The path to this family had almost cost her life but the acceptance and love the Matthews were capable of sharing was unquantifiable. She leaned into Carole's shoulder. "I'm glad you're here. Thank you."

Carole kissed her temple. "How long have you been on the floor? Do you think we can stand up and be more comfortable?"

Argia remained silent but her hands tightened the clumps of Noreen's shirt she clung to. Noreen kissed her forehead. "Gia, honey, Grammy's right. It could be dark for a long time. Let's have a pajama party in your room, just the three of us. We'll all squeeze into your bed and have ice cream. How would you like that?" Argia remained unresponsive.

"That's a great idea," Carole said. "We'll even let Mr. Fox and Mr. Dog have a cup. C'mon, darling, let's help Noreen off the floor. We don't want her leg hurt again." She rolled to her knees and stood, bending over to coax Noreen onto her knees and then grasping her beneath the armpits and helping her stand with Argia cradled against her. Carole crinkled her nose at the whiff of urine, but Noreen just shook her head. It didn't matter if Argia peed on her. It would likely be years before either one of them stopped fearing the dark.

Carole gathered the flashlights and led the way to Argia's room. She tightened the bedspread and patted it invitingly. Noreen climbed onto the bed and settled Argia on her lap. "Relax, honey, we're safe in your room. Grammy is here with us. We're going to have ice cream."

Carole's voice drifted in from the kitchen and Noreen surmised she'd called Blake. "Yes, I'm here. I'll stay as long as I need to, don't worry. She's pretty frightened but Noreen has her. Don't worry, I have enough TLC for both of them. Okay, I'll tell them. I love you too."

Carole returned with three scented candles in glass containers that she positioned on Argia's bookshelf, nightstand, and windowsill. "I just talked to your daddy. I told him we're having a PJ party with ice cream. He said he loves you both very much."

A wave of warmth coursed through Noreen. Blake wasn't shy about professing his feelings for her. Carole left and returned with five cups of ice cream on a dinner plate, one each for Mr. Fox and Mr. Dog as promised. Noreen shifted sideways and Carole sat beside her.

"Ice cream for everyone, Gia. If Mr. Dog and Mr. Fox won't eat theirs, you'll have to. What does Grammy always tell you? Ice cream makes everything better."

At last, Gia rolled her head away from Noreen's chest and eyed her grandmother. Carole peeled the lid off one cup, plunged a teaspoon into it, and extended it toward Argia. Two flashlights shined from the foot of the bed, casting them in silhouettes.

Noreen shut her eyes tight. This wasn't the nightmare resurrecting itself. She was safe. She leaned back, willing herself to relax so Gia felt her muscles release. "Let's have some ice cream, honey, and then it will be your bedtime. We can all sleep here together until morning."

Eyes as round as poker chips stared at her. "Will Daddy be here in the morning?"

Just the thought lightened her heart and she smiled. "You bet he will. And he has two days off to spend with us. I bet he'll want ice cream too."

Gia shifted ever so slightly and reached for the treat. Noreen repositioned her between her legs, raising both to form a cocoon and accepted her cup of ice cream from Carole. Gia spooned some into her mouth and offered a taste to Mr. Dog.

Once the ice cream was gone, Argia crawled back onto her lap, gathering her stuffed friends in her arms, and tugging on her special blanket to draw a corner over her shoulder. The blankey that she loaned Noreen to pad her leg when it was broken wasn't salvageable, having been ripped, singed, and blackened beyond laundering. She'd kept it beneath her leg in the hospital while recovering and convinced Argia that she didn't always have to carry the blanket with her animals. Eventually, Argia consented to a new blanket, which most of the time stayed on her bed. It was a big concession for Gia that Blake credited Noreen with enabling.

She wasn't sure what time they fell asleep. The stress of the blackout had exhausted them both. She woke when Blake kissed her forehead.

"Good morning. You're beautiful when you sleep, do you know that?"

She smiled. "You're beautiful to wake up to." She shifted, careful not to disturb Argia asleep by her side. Sunlight spilled in from the window. "Are the lights back on?"

"Yeah, about an hour ago." Blake crinkled his nose. "Why do you smell like pee?"

"Gia had an accident when your mom rang the bell. I didn't want to let her go so I couldn't change. Did your mom leave?"

"No, she's in the kitchen making breakfast. C'mon." Blake took her hand and waited while she slid off the bed. Gia curled into a ball and Blake drew the covers up to her shoulders. She didn't awaken.

After a whiff of herself, Noreen coughed.

"Do I have time for a shower?"

Blake grinned. "That's my plan." He led her to the master bedroom and closed the door. Before she could protest, Blake drew her into his arms and covered her mouth with his. All angst from the previous night dissolved in his embrace, his tongue whisking away any minutes of fear. He lifted her shirt over her head and unhooked her bra, allowing both to fall to the floor. His fingers brushed across the scars on her back and for one brief second, she stiffened. But this man knew the origin of those injuries, still felt somewhat responsible for Lynne's attack and abduction of her and Argia, and reassured her with his words and actions that although marred on the surface, she was perfect in his eyes.

While he wrestled with the snap on her jeans, she unbuttoned his uniform shirt, eager to touch his massive chest and feel his taut skin against hers. Once they were both naked, Blake led her to the walk-in shower and drew her underneath the jet. This was how it felt to be loved by the man, doused from head to toe in heat, saturated like a wildfire he might battle and hope to tame. But there was no taming their passion.

As warm water cascaded over them, they groped and soaped and strained for the connection that only sex can make. Blake sat on the built-in ledge and urged her to straddle him and find nirvana.

In minutes, she climaxed and Blake followed. Then they clung to each other, breathing hard, kissing harder, whispering their feelings.

She'd never make the mistake Lynne Matthews made. Never would she let this man go.

8

"Oh my goodness, Blake, what's your mother going to think?"

Breathless, Noreen rose from his lap and reached for her sea sponge. Blake rested his shoulders against the tile wall, his eyes still closed.

"She's going to think that I can't keep my hands off you, which is a fact she already knows. I told her we were going to jump in the shower."

"I'm sure she didn't think you meant together." She flicked water in his face when he grinned and shrugged. "Get a move on. I'm hungry. And Gia will likely want to crawl under your shirt and keep close to you all day."

"I plan to keep you both close. Was it bad last night?"

She swallowed hard. "I'm glad your mom came over. I'm not strong in the dark."

"You're the strongest woman I know."

Goosebumps prickled her skin when he stood and began to lather his torso. She'd never tire of seeing him naked. The tattoo of Gia's birthdate on his chest below the tribal design that spilled down his shoulder and upper arm still aroused her. She averted her attention.

He was a magnificent being. Dark hair covered his long, muscular legs. Thick thighs and washboard abs were evidence of hours spent lifting weights and logging his daily running miles. Shoulder muscles like thick electrical cords. She could identify each part of him medically. Quadriceps. Abductors. Soleus. And his fine gluteals. Deltoids. Sculpted pectoral muscles beneath a smattering of hair. Yeah, she could easily rattle off the medical identification of all his parts.

She preferred identifying him by touch and taste.

Living with Blake was supposed to be temporary while she recuperated. But if healing meant moving out, she didn't want to ever get well.

She'd spent five weeks in the hospital after Lynne lured her to the Matthews' former home, shoved her down the cellar steps, breaking her leg in the process, and locked both her and Argia in an underground room. She'd left them to die, Noreen had no doubt. Had Lynne been smart enough to keep her cool, Blake and his squad might never have found them.

Noreen's broken leg required surgery and the burns on her back and shoulders necessitated daily attention. Once her doctors released her from the hospital, Blake insisted she stay at the house he rented in Plum Borough, an upscale suburb of Pittsburgh. His mother lived in the same community, on the opposite end. Blake convinced her that he, his mother, and Gia could take care of her broken, burned, and battered body.

About the only thing that hadn't hurt was her heart. Blake and Gia filled it with love. In the months of therapy and convalescence that followed, the three of them became a family and Noreen never moved back to her apartment. When the lease expired, Blake asked her not to renew.

He swatted her playfully on the bottom before leaving the bedroom. "What are you lollygagging about? Throw on some clothes, woman, before I ravish you again. I'll see if Gia is awake."

Laughing, she switched on the hair dryer and aimed it at him. "Then stop distracting me." It hadn't been her intention to stay. But leaving those two was impossible. Light had become an important commodity to her, and Blake and Gia lit up her life. She'd never allow darkness to prevail again.

BLAKE silently nudged open his daughter's bedroom door expecting Gia to still be asleep. Since the blinds hadn't been closed the night before, the early morning sun filled the room in shades of yellow. His precious Gia lay in her "big girl bed" with the covers drawn to her chin, her fingers pinched white holding tight, her eyes wide open. Mr. Fox and Mr. Dog peeked out from the covers too, also wide-eyed and staring at him, although Mr. Fox's glare was a little lopsided ever since he'd had his head sewn back on.

"Hey Peanut, are you awake?" He crept to the side of the bed, drew back the blanket and slipped in beside her, bending his legs to fit and drawing Gia into the nest his body formed. She was shaking.

"Hey? What's the matter? Did you have a bad dream?"

Eyes as round as saucers stared at him. She shook her head, her bottom lip protruding slightly. Dammit, she was back in silent mode. He kissed her forehead. "Not talking to me this morning? How come? You mad at me?"

She shook her head again. "Well then how come the silent treatment?"

Sometimes he could nudge her into responding. "It makes Daddy sad when I don't hear your lovely voice. If something is wrong, you have to tell me so I can fix it."

His heart cracked when tears filled her eyes. She whispered,

"I was ascared, Daddy. I tinkled on Weenie. Remember how Mother would holler when I had a accident? What if Weenie doesn't love me now?"

Blake wrestled with the range of emotions engulfing him. Gia hadn't referenced her mother since the fire, and he'd wondered what horrors filled her head. Obviously, she remembered that Lynne insisted on being called Mother, a title he hated. But he hated that she referred to herself as The Captain too. Did Gia harbor fears that Noreen would treat her like Lynne had if she stepped out of line? Lynne was a monster. Noreen was incapable of such ugliness.

He brushed the hair off Gia's forehead, not wanting to diminish what for her was real anguish. "I don't think you have to worry about that, pumpkin. Accidents happen. Noreen isn't mad at you for that. When I came home this morning, she was asleep right here beside you, holding on to you real tight." He pressed the blankets on either side to tighten them. "I had to pry her fingers loose. I didn't think she'd ever let go of you."

At least that produced half a smile. "Where is she then?"

Moments ago, she'd been in his arms, loving him like there was no tomorrow. His jeans tightened at the recollection. "She's taking a shower. And Grammy is making breakfast so we should get you up and dressed too."

Gia's fingers tightened on the blankets. He knew his daughter like he knew himself. Something else troubled her. He kissed the tip of her nose and leveled his gaze on her, diving into her psyche, reaching for her soul. This was their special way to communicate, just the two of them. A link from body to body, mind to mind and heart to heart, as if they heard each other's thoughts, read each other's minds. "Tell me," he whispered.

"I'm ascared, Daddy."

His heart splintered a fraction more. Would his darling

baby girl ever not be afraid after what she'd endured? "Tell Daddy what scares you."

Her lips moved ever so slightly, then clamped tight. Blake cocked his head and whispered, "No fair, Gia. You know you can tell me anything. What are you afraid of, Peanut?" He leaned in and turned his ear to hear and even then, he barely captured the word.

"Mother."

She was six years old but smart enough to realize they hadn't extricated Lynne from their lives yet. He couldn't share that he was afraid too, fearful of Lynne's plans to ruin their happiness and doubtful of a judicial system that placed a higher value on a mother's rights than a child's well-being. Gia had witnessed him almost kill her mother. In fact, her tiny fists pounding his thighs and her screams to stop were what kept him from choking Lynne to death. Gia hadn't saved Lynne that night, she'd saved him.

Inhaling deeply, he weighed his words. How could he reassure Gia that her mother, who tried to kill her once already, wouldn't hurt her again when he didn't believe it himself?

"Your mom is sick, honey. She's trying to get better. She won't ever hurt you again, though, that I promise." He tapped her chest. "You and me, Gia, we're a team. We stay together no matter what. Don't doubt that for a second. I know you don't like to think about what your mom did but remember how hard Daddy searched for you? Remember how Noreen took care of you and made sure you got out of that house? That's never going to change. We're always going to protect you and take care of you. In fact, you're never going to be allowed to have boyfriends or go away to college, get married or even be out of my sight for too long. That's how much I love you."

He hoped for a giggle but she wasn't calmed.

"What if she takes me away from you, Daddy?"

Noreen's voice surprised them both. "I won't let that

happen." He hadn't heard her in the doorway. How long had she been standing there?

She didn't step into the room. Noreen respected his time with Gia, always giving them their space together. Lynne had never understood their connection, resented their closeness, and tried to insert herself into their bond.

Noreen wasn't threatened by his relationship with Gia. Instead of trying to come between them, she folded them both into her heart. His face erupted in a wide grin just looking at her. He'd loved his ex-wife at first. He couldn't describe what he felt for Noreen. The rush was so powerful, it weakened him.

He returned his attention to Gia. "There. You see? Nothing to worry about. I'm not going to let your mother have you and neither is Noreen."

"Promise?"

How to convince her she was safe? "Cross my heart. I promise."

Gia turned to look at Noreen and when she moved her fingers over her heart to outline a cross, his heart exploded with love for her. "I promise. Breakfast is ready. If you two don't hurry up, I'm going to eat all the Mickey Mouse pancakes myself." She blew them a kiss and closed the door, leaving them to their morning ritual.

"Let's throw you in the tub for a quick rinse. You can take a long bubble bath later, okay? We'll get you dressed and go eat some breakfast." He withdrew the covers and helped Gia out of bed.

"You promised, Daddy, and I believe you." They walked hand in hand to the bathroom. "But I'm still ascared."

9

Lynne feared her plan hadn't worked. But lo and behold, these anal men who couldn't take their eyes off her legs crossed beneath her fitted pencil skirt or her breasts overflowing her push-up bra and straining the buttons on her blouse, were agreeing to her release date. All she had to do was demonstrate progress with her daughter.

Without Blake in the room, that should be easy. Her attorney had successfully argued that Blake impeded her reconnection with Argia. He was barred from the meeting room while she visited.

The chairman of the review board flipped through the pages of her file. "You've displayed remarkable progress, Mrs. Matthews. Your doctor raves about his sessions with you. Your mental and social adjustments exceed his expectations."

That quack of a psychiatrist was as simple as this panel, easily duped by a tease. He never caught on that she dropped something every session and had to bend over to retrieve it, always displaying her cleavage. His attraction toward her was his first mistake. Underestimating her was the second.

"I see here the only completed box still unchecked in your

files is a re-established relationship with your daughter. Would you elaborate about that for us? Is there an issue we're unaware of?"

She sat up straighter and thrust out her chest. "No, not at all. Certainly nothing that is insurmountable once I can spend time with her in a home environment." She spread her hands, palms open. "While every attempt is taken to make Dalton House feel like home, it's a lot to ask a child to understand, let alone accept. She's only six, gentlemen. She's been spoiled by her father since I haven't been around to serve as the disciplinarian so naturally, she's somewhat rebellious when she's expected to mind her mother. I'm confident I can undo any bad habits her father has allowed her to adopt. She's visiting me this afternoon without him, and I expect the whole tone of the session will be positive. I'm looking forward to holding her."

Blake's lawyer had fought hard against restricting Blake from the room, but the judge was lenient and ruled in favor of Lynne's rights as a mother working to reclaim reintegration into society and her family. She would've loved to see Blake's face when he received that news. He wouldn't be permitted beyond the front gate today. The receptionist would meet Argia at the front door to take her to the family room and Fran would supervise the hour.

The chairman nodded. "Ah, good. Yours is a model case for this state-funded rehabilitation program. If today's session is constructive, I see no reason why you can't continue your treatment as an outpatient. We've reviewed the terms of your probation and they accommodate your treatment. You're well on your way to move forward with your life."

The urge to stand and applaud swept over her. Instead, she strived to look demure when she lowered her gaze to the table and whispered, "I'm so grateful for the chance to rebuild my life and take back what I surrendered. My own home. My privacy. My independence." Silently, she added her husband to that list, but these goons didn't need to know that.

They consulted a calendar, agreed on a tentative date when she could walk out of this hellhole, contingent on the success of today's session, and wished her luck. She strode to her room to retrieve the new baby doll Phillip had purchased, following her exact directions. She'd searched pages and pages on the library computer for just the right one.

What little girl wouldn't want a new dolly? She wouldn't force Argia onto her lap, she'd make her come to her for the gift. Her step was light as she walked toward the private visiting room, catching Fran's eye when she passed her office. "It's almost time for Argia. I'm so excited I want to be in the room waiting."

Fran smiled, nodded, and rose to follow her. Lynne opened the door, stopped in her tracks, and screamed. The shriek echoed through the hall, prompting a few residents to peek out of their doors to see what was happening. Her body temperature hiked to stroke level and the heat that engulfed her face likely turned her skin fire engine red. This was a new level of rage.

Argia sat on Noreen Jensen's lap, those filthy stuffed toys pressed to her chest, crushing the ruffles on her cucumber green dress. Her daughter refused to look at her, instead her eyes downcast to the floor. But that cold-hearted whore-nurse leveled ice cube orbs on her.

Fran had been following so close behind, she walked into Lynne's back and bounced backward. She peered over Lynne's shoulder just as Lynne exploded. "How dare you? What are you doing here?" She pointed to the door. "Get out! Get out this instant. You are in direct violation of a court-ordered private visit with my daughter." She turned to Fran, whose brows knit in confusion. "Call security. This woman has no right being here. Call them now."

She spun around to confront Noreen again. "What are you still doing here? I said get out."

Argia had shriveled into a small ball, her feet drawn up and her face buried in the stuffed animals. Noreen slid a printed page across the table.

"I have every right to be here. The court order specifically restricts Blake Matthews from this visit. I am not Blake Matthews. There's a copy if you'd like to read it."

A security guard stepped into the room. Lynne had seen the rent-a-cops walking the perimeter of the property at various times during the day and night. They weren't armed and she doubted they had much authority. But it was worth a shot.

She addressed him. "This woman has no right to interfere with a private visit with my daughter. She's violating a court order. I want her removed immediately."

He reached for the page Noreen provided and Fran read over his shoulder. Lynne fired more volleys. "The court specifically redefined the terms of my parental visits. The father is excluded, and a qualified staff member must supervise the private visit. Fran is here in that supervisory capacity. Must I remind you that private means just me and my daughter? This woman needs to leave. Now."

Her angered heightened when Noreen ignored her and produced more documents for the rent-a-cop. "Here is a copy of the original court order establishing the requirements for Lynne Matthews' meetings with her daughter. You'll see it permits the child's father or legal guardian to be present for all interactions, including telephonic. She is correct when she references an amended court order restricting Blake Matthews from participating in today's visit. I have it here. The judge's order only pertains to Mr. Matthews."

Her vision blurred with outrage. Noreen reached into her bag and retrieved another printed sheet, which she extended to the guard. "If you'll read this, sir, you'll see it identifies me as a legal guardian for Argia Matthews in her father's absence where exigent circumstances exist. It's signed by Blake Matthews and notarized. I have copies if you'd like them for your files."

Lynne snatched the paper from his hand, barely able to focus on the wording. "What exigent circumstances? This is outrageous."

The guard cleared his throat. "Uh, what do you mean exigent?"

Lynne suppressed her retort. Was he stupid? And then her internal thermometer exploded. She looked at her arms, certain that her blood started to curdle and bubble beneath her skin when she watched the whore-nurse tighten her arms around *her* daughter. This was unacceptable. This was the reason Noreen Jensen needed to die.

Noreen nodded. "The definition of exigent, as I'm sure you know, is a situation or circumstance that requires more than is reasonable. Let's not forget what brings Mrs. Matthews to this facility in the first place. Abduction charges."

Her words couldn't come out loud enough. "How dare you?" Argia jerked and whimpered. But no one seemed to notice, their attention on her.

Her indignation choked her. How dare this woman bring up false facts. "Those charges were bogus and were reduced. And I...I—" The guard held up his hand to stop her tirade.

Argia may have been intimidated, but Noreen was unshaken, staring at her without blinking. She should have finished her off in that damn basement.

Noreen kept her focus on the guard, as if she weren't standing beside him ready to implode. Dismissing her. What nerve. *She* was Argia's mother.

"It is our position that any personal interaction between Argia and her mother is an exigent circumstance that requires the presence of her father or, in his absence, her legal guardian.

I believe Mr. Matthews' lawyer filed a brief this morning supporting this opinion and challenging the judge's decision to forbid him from participating. In the spirit of cooperation, Mr. Matthews deemed it unreasonable to cancel today's visit while the attorneys argue a point of law. Since Mrs. Matthews made it impossible for Mr. Matthews to be here, I'm legally here on his behalf."

The guard coughed. "Do you have some identification?"

Lynne's chest heaved. "This is absurd. I know who she is. She has no rights. She's nothing to Argia." She stiffened when Argia turned and wrapped her arms around Noreen, burying her face in Noreen's neck.

The guard shrugged. "This all looks legal, ma'am." Behind him, Fran nodded. "This gives her the right to be here. I suggest you make the best of it and enjoy a visit with your daughter." He dropped the paper on the table and strode to the door. She turned her rage on Fran. "Don't just stand there. Say something."

Fran's shoulders drooped. "It's all in order, Lynne. You specifically filed against your husband, not this woman. I think—"

"Ex-husband," Noreen interrupted. "She's no longer married to Mr. Matthews."

Lynne drew in a full breath like a dragon preparing to breathe fire, but Fran squeezed her arm hard enough to bruise. "Remember how much you have riding on this session." Her eyes darted toward the observation camera in the corner and then back to Lynne's face. "You're allotted one hour. I think you should use the rest of your time wisely."

She seethed. This was the ultimate insult, watching Blake's whore cradle her daughter and worse, seeing Argia cling to her. It was one more nail in Noreen Jensen's coffin. Hoping to convey her hatred, she bore into the woman's eyes with a look she wished could kill.

Noreen's heart raced so fast, she fought with her body to breathe. A cement block on her chest couldn't weigh more. Gia likely felt it pounding against her own chest. The child was pressed against her, trembling.

But she didn't blink, didn't dare look away from Lynne's deadly stare. If this was a battle of wills, she wasn't backing down. She'd bested this woman once. She could do it again.

All the reason she needed to win shuddered in her arms.

This was the first time she'd come face-to-face with Lynne since that night in the hospital, when Lynne tried to smother her. She'd fought like a wild woman and then watched in horror when Blake tried to choke Lynne to death. She wanted her dead that night, even while she screamed for Blake to stop. She'd been grateful Joe and the others arrived in time but sorry that Lynne lived to threaten them now.

She'd glimpsed the real Lynne Matthews that night, a hideous, heartless attempted murderer.

The plea deals negotiated between the authorities and medical experts seemed to go on forever, with Blake returning home after each meeting angry and reaching for his scotch. The final agreement negated the need for a trial. And only Blake had attended the adjudication hearing.

Mostly wanting an end to it all so they could move forward with their lives, Blake had agreed to reduced charges, psychiatric help, and a newly launched state rehabilitation project. Lost in the fine print was the insertion of Lynne back into their lives, disguised as monitored transition. The mother and daughter reunions were a dreadful failure.

In preparation for today's visit, Blake had described the process, the staff she'd encounter, and this meeting area, which was an attempt by Dalton House to create a familial setting. An overstuffed sofa beneath a window in one corner was crowded by shelves loaded with games and books and a large area rug. An unfinished Lego castle sat in the middle of the carpet.

A day bed with stuffed toys in all sizes and bright pillows in all shapes atop a bright animal print blanket occupied the opposite corner. Blake had suggested Noreen and Gia sit at the two-person round table in a third corner, designed as an efficient kitchen area. A small refrigerator, coffee pot, and cookie jar sat on the Formica counter. Sitting at the table strategically kept a piece of furniture between them and Lynne. The couch or loveseat allowed too much proximity, in his opinion.

Thankfully, she'd followed his advice. The chair wasn't the most comfortable, but the table felt like a life preserver. Watching Lynne's fists clench and her chest rise and fall, the barrier between them created a sense of boundary.

Argia clung to her so tightly, her clothes were damp from the intense body heat. She tightened her hold on the child, who quaked as if she sat in a meat locker, and eyed the woman Blake had once proclaimed undying love for. It was difficult to comprehend.

Despite her heaving chest, the pulsing veins in her neck and blood-red face, Lynne looked beautiful. Her charcoal gray pants suit was tailored to accentuate her figure. She was thinner than Noreen remembered. The stitching on the jacket was designed to flatter her breasts. Noreen didn't recall those being as buxom. The cream-colored blouse beneath the jacket softened her skin, which as always, appeared flawless. Not a hair was out of place today. Dark red lips. Eye makeup applied as if done by a professional.

But beneath those false lashes, Lynne's dark eyes—the eyes she'd given Gia—were empty. There was no soul evident. Only evil.

Noreen no longer deemed herself inferior to this fiend. Ugliness festered just beneath Lynne's perfect cosmetic surface.

Lynne fought hard to control that beast now, taking deep

breaths, flexing her fists open and closed. Her eyes narrowed to menacing slits, and her glossed lips pressed tight. Fran grabbed her arm and cautioned her. Too bad. Noreen was itching for a confrontation with the monster, one that the security cameras could capture to reveal the true Lynne Matthews.

She'd dialed Blake before entering this room with Gia and kept the line open, leaving her phone sit on the table. She glanced at the wall clock. That was almost twenty minutes ago. Only forty more.

Blake and Joe waited outside listening to every word. Recalling the conversation the day before between Blake and Joe, she smiled. "If there's trouble and we need to storm in there, I'm going down for it," Joe had insisted. "We can't afford to take you out of the game."

Her smile caught Lynne's attention. Her shoulders squared and she yanked her arm out of the counselor's grip. "Do you find this funny, Noreen?"

Blake had warned not to let Lynne bait her. She didn't plan to engage in a debate, but her grin widened.

Exasperated at her lack of response, Lynne bent to retrieve a baby doll from the floor. She hadn't noticed it in Lynne's hands when she walked in, or saw it drop. Lynne straightened the doll's dress and adjusted one crooked shoe. Her voice softened and she extended it toward them.

"Argia? Look at the nice surprise Mother has for you. A sweet new baby doll. Look, Argia, she's wearing a dress with ruffles just like yours."

Tiny fingers dug into the backs of Noreen's arms.

"This is ludicrous," Lynne spat at Fran. "I can't communicate with my daughter while this, this, bit—this woman influences her to ignore me. She's not even looking at me, for God's sake. This is exactly the objection I have regarding her father. My daughter is not free to display any affection toward me with her here."

Noreen ignored the counselor's response and whispered to Argia. "Gia, honey, please for me, turn around and face your mother. You don't have to speak, just turn in my lap. We both want to get out of here, but we can't if you don't turn around. I promise not to let you go."

"Promise?" She barely heard the pitiful plea.

Noreen kissed the top of Argia's head, causing Lynne to hiss when she caught her breath. "I promise."

Argia sat up and her tear-streaked face broke Noreen's heart. No child should be tortured like this. Squeezing the life out of Mr. Dog and Mr. Fox, she moved her legs toward Noreen's knees and with help, swiveled until she faced Lynne. Noreen checked the clock again. Only a half-hour longer. They could do this.

Standing behind Lynne, Fran smiled. Who could resist smiling at Argia's round, cherub face, those long lashes over dark chocolate eyes and that toothy grin? Except Noreen doubted Gia was smiling.

Lynne strolled to a rocking chair and dragged it closer. Argia bristled when she stopped four feet from them and sat. "There, that's better," Lynne cooed. "My sweet girl, look what I have for you." She shook the doll. "Wouldn't you like to play with her instead of those dirty stuffed toys? Come over here and I'll play with you."

Argia smashed Mr. Fox and Mr. Dog to her chest. Noreen straightened Gia's dress and patted her thighs.

"Really, Argia, I know you want this doll. I see you peeking at it. I have some extra clothes for her too so you can dress and undress her, just like Mother does with you."

She sensed her eyebrows rise. Blake was the parent who regularly dressed and fed Argia when he and Lynne were married. It was why his thick fingers easily manipulated tiny buttons and snaps and hair ribbons. Her stomach quivered. He could work magic with those fingers.

"Argia!"

She and Argia both jumped. Blake had instructed her not to interfere if possible. There was nothing to stop Lynne from petitioning the judge to also exclude Noreen from the visits. But a long line of people waited to be designated legal guardian next, starting with Carole Matthews, Joe and Brittni, Kelly, and every man on Blake's squad. She and Blake were surprised by that kind of support, and comforted.

Noreen's patience was teetering. Seven more minutes. She hadn't saved this child's life to allow her mother to torment her.

"Gia," she whispered, "do you want the doll?"

An empathic head shake no.

Lynne shoved the doll forward in the air. "I bought it for her. I want her to have it. A little girl needs a decent toy, not some ratty pieces of cloth. Argia, take the doll. Now."

"I'm sorry, Lynne, she doesn't seem interested in it. And it looks like our hour is about up." She coaxed Argia off her lap and stood, dropping her phone in her blazer pocket. Argia hid behind her leg, her face buried against her back thigh.

Lynne catapulted out of the seat. "You can't take her away from me. I'll have you arrested." Fran rushed to her side and reminded her of the cameras.

Lynne's attitude changed immediately, and the word psychopath popped into Noreen's head.

Did the cameras capture audio as well as video? Lynne certainly didn't sound calm and rehabilitated.

"All right, Argia, maybe you'll want the doll next time. I'll be getting out of here soon and we'll have a nicer place to be together. You'll have your own room. And Mother will take good care of you."

Argia tugged on Noreen's pant leg, raised her hands and Noreen lifted the child into her arms, nestling the stuffed animals against her chest. She'd crawled through fire with Mr. Fox tucked in her bra. He likely felt right at home there. And holding Gia, protecting her from the beast who stood before them, who'd tried to kill them, was as natural as blinking. She turned toward the door.

"Noreen!"

She pivoted to face Lynne again.

"This isn't over. Don't think you've won. She's my child."

Argia's arms tightened around her neck. "Biologically, perhaps. But they both belong to me now. And you already know what I'll do to protect them."

10

Outside Dalton House, Blake paced in front of Joe who leaned against his truck holding the phone level like a dinner plate so they could listen to what went on inside. "I think she's leaving. Sounds like footsteps."

Blake spun to stare at the front entrance and rushed to the gate when Noreen emerged carrying Gia. Arms extended, Gia fell into his embrace and he crushed her to his chest. Joe gave Noreen a brief hug and wrapped his arm around her waist, escorting her to Blake's truck. Blake reached to caress her cheek.

"You did fine. Thank God we have you." He leaned in to kiss her mouth and felt her lips quaking. "It's okay. Come here." Moving Gia to his right hip, he drew Noreen to his side. She was shaking like a paint mixer machine. "It's over now, you're safe. God, I love you." Gia wrapped her arm around Noreen's neck. "Love you, Weenie."

She lifted her face to look at him and tears glistened in her eyes. Yet she stood strong for him and his daughter. Since the day he'd met her, she'd protected her patients—her children—

like a mother cub. "I love you both, too. Can we get away from here?"

Joe suggested the three of them ride in the back seat while he drove, and they huddled together as if rescued from a sinking ship. Gia surprised him by crawling onto Noreen's lap when they climbed inside. Noreen yanked the seatbelt across both of them and snapped it tight, then wrapped her arms around Gia's tiny frame. Since being under his constant care—his and Noreen's—Gia was eating better and had gained weight. But she still ranked in the bottom third on the growth chart.

Joe spoke to the rearview mirror. "How about the three of you come over to our place. We can have a drink, relax, and figure out what to do next. Brittni is planning dinner."

He didn't feel much like eating, but he sure could use a drink. "Thanks, Joey, but this isn't your concern." Noreen's hand slid into his.

Joe laughed. "We may not be blood related, Lewey, but we're brothers. We'll do what we do at the station. Sit around the table and hash it out."

Blake grinned despite his sour mood. He could use a session around the Table of Trust, the kitchen table his squad gathered around to discuss, debate, argue, confide, and resolve any question or issue they had as a team or individually. Everyone was equal, which was why no one ever sat at the head of the table. All comments were offered and welcomed without judgment.

Usually, Blake maintained a social distance from the members of his unit, hesitant to become too friendly with men he might have to reprimand. But since the abduction and fire last summer, when his men rallied around him to search for Gia and surveil Lynne 24/7, he'd formed a new bond with them, especially Joe. He turned toward Noreen wondering if she was up for the visit and she nodded.

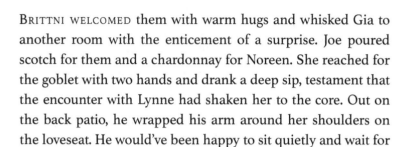

BRITTNI WELCOMED them with warm hugs and whisked Gia to another room with the enticement of a surprise. Joe poured scotch for them and a chardonnay for Noreen. She reached for the goblet with two hands and drank a deep sip, testament that the encounter with Lynne had shaken her to the core. Out on the back patio, he wrapped his arm around her shoulders on the loveseat. He would've been happy to sit quietly and wait for dinner. But Joey had an agenda.

"As I understand it, even when Lynne is released, her time with Gia still has to be supervised, right?"

"Yes, but what's to stop her from standing outside the school yard or knocking on the door when Noreen and I are both on duty and Brittni is there alone? I know Brittni would never let Lynne inside, but she could still make a hell of a scene on the front porch and Gia would hear it all."

"What about a restraining order so she can't come that close?"

He shrugged. "She has to do something offensive first to warrant one."

Joe blew out a loud breath. "Kidnapping, attempted murder and arson aren't offensive?"

It was the catch-22 predicament they were in, just like before. The Munchausen Syndrome by Proxy argument was deflated by Lynne's claim of diminished mental capacity. He'd been unable to prove any of the disasters were deliberate up to the abduction and fire. And there'd been no proof who actually set the fire that almost killed Noreen and Gia.

Assault charges related to the attack on Noreen and her injuries had been pleaded down in legal maneuvers that still baffled him. How can you throw someone down a flight of stairs, severely injuring them, and not face consequences? No matter how many ways his lawyer explained the plea deal, he didn't like it. But he'd agreed to it, hoping to end the whole mess.

"My attorney is searching for another lawful avenue to pursue." Even he could hear the lack of enthusiasm in that sentence. He was a proactive man, not someone who waited to react. This feeling of helplessness unnerved him. He gulped the remainder of his scotch.

The rustle of tulle and Gia's happy squeal caught everyone's attention when she skipped into the room wearing a sparkly tiara and a gold princess dress. Belle. Yeah, she was the yellow one. He knew this one. Gia spun in a circle and then threw herself into his lap. "Daddy, daddy, look, I'm a princess. Make a wish and I can make it come true."

How he wished she could.

He cupped her rosy cheeks with his hands. "Daddy wishes for twofers from his princess."

Gia giggled and promptly kissed him on his left cheek, right cheek, forehead, and lips, counting each peck as she delivered it. "One. Two. One. Two."

She danced over to Noreen and his heart leapt. His sweet baby girl was happy again. He wouldn't let anything or anyone ruin that.

While Noreen laid her finger on her chin and stared at the sky trying to think of a wish, he excused himself to answer his ringing phone and frowned when he saw it was his home security company. And then he swore. Someone had tried to break into the house.

11

R age simmered below Lynne's skin like a pot about to boil. Not rolling in full force but occasionally bubbling, circulating, heating up slowly. Her hands were always fisted, even as she sat in the common room enjoying social hour with her housemates. Or at least pretending to.

Every so often she had to unclench her teeth to relax her jaw. Spread her fingers wide and clasp her hands behind her back to release the tension in her neck. It rarely worked.

Her spine never relaxed against the chair, but she couldn't stand without pacing. Her voice had an edge to it in every response she offered to even the most mundane questions, her vocal cords stiff like stretched guitar strings. At night she punched her pillows seeking a comfortable position to sleep, kicked off the covers and then drew them to her chin, flopped on her belly then twisted to recline on her back where a knot the size of a plum stayed wedged between her shoulder blades.

She was a ticking time bomb in the human sense. Angry at the world. Mad at herself for screwing up when she had the chance to dispose of Noreen Jensen. Livid that Blake had outsmarted her. Annoyed that Fran and that worthless rent-a-cop hadn't sided with her, had let that whore-nurse manhandle her daughter. Fuming that *that woman* lived with Argia and Blake. Furious that Noreen Jensen lived at all.

She should be celebrating that she was leaving this house. Transitioning to independent living. Instead, all she wanted was to break something. Or hurt somebody.

That damn lawyer that Blake hired convinced some weakling judge that she should not be left alone with her child. No overnight visits. No mother-daughter moments. A legal guardian must always be present. Not Blake. The judge conceded his presence was adversely influential on Argia. But someone of Blake's choosing would monitor.

Phillip said it wasn't a big deal. He'd called it a bump in the road and assured Lynne she could overcome it. He saw the court decision as a boon for her goal. In his mind, it placed Noreen Jensen right in her hands. All Lynne had to do was throw Noreen off balance. She'd done it before. It was a mountain she was making out of an anthill.

How could he look at it so logically?

A man couldn't comprehend the bond that forms between a mother and her child while in the womb. Phillip didn't get it. Of course, he'd never met Argia so he didn't understand how delicate she was. She was a frail child who needed her mother's protection, not some whore-nurse who likely brought home every germ imaginable from the hospital every day.

There was an upside, though, to his not knowing her. Without Argia around, Phillip doted on her. Blake had idolized her too, before Argia came along. Then it was all she could do to get his attention.

Inexplicably, Argia had a way of winning everyone over. She'd have to keep the kid in check this time, maybe semi-drugged. She wouldn't be displaced again, and she wouldn't let the little snot wheedle her way into Phillip's good graces and play second fiddle to the brat a second time.

It might be easier to give up the fight. Truthfully, she didn't like tending to Argia. The child required too much attention and infringed on Lynne's time for herself. She'd had to lock her in the closet as a baby just to soak in the tub.

But giving up would mean Noreen won. And she'd be damned if she'd let that happen.

She tossed her belongings into her designer tote, not bothering to fold her clothes or protect them from her street shoes. She'd be throwing them all out anyway and buying new. Anything that reminded her of this place was history. Phillip should be arriving in less than an hour to drive her away from this prison. Hopefully, he was as horny as she was.

She'd met him last spring in the auto parts store across town from their home. Well, the home she used to share with Blake. She'd wandered in looking for some kind of tracker, not knowing exactly what she shopped for but certain the black leather mini skirt, knee-high boots and sheer silk blouse would result in assistance from someone who comprehended what she described. The teenager behind the counter had shrugged when she inquired about "a device to follow people with," said the store didn't carry anything like that, and advised her to search online. That would leave a paper trail. Too traceable.

"I must not be describing it correctly. It's one of those locator gizmos that I see advertised. Surely you have something like that."

But the acned-faced boy was too busy on his phone to do more than shake his head. Frustrated, she turned away from the counter and saw Phillip wave to her.

He'd noticed her when she walked in, lifting his chin, and tapping the brim of his ball cap as she passed. She'd taken a deep breath and thrust out her chest to make sure. She'd bet a thousand bucks he was drooling at the rear view too. After he signaled her, she approached slowly, gauging each step, allowing time for his eyes to roam the length of her body. A seductive walk of wiles that he fully comprehended. His appraisal sent an anticipatory shiver down her spine. He motioned her to the next aisle.

By the look on his face, his glazed over eyes, he liked what he saw. Nothing boosted her confidence like a man's obvious desire. Her three-inch heels brought him to eye level. He was rough around the edges, his beard unkempt, his fingernails dirty, but his jeans were tight and his smile was white. She hated yellowed teeth.

The game of meeting and toying with a new man was an exciting challenge. Her heart pounded.

He cleared his throat, dragging his gaze from her breasts to her face. "I couldn't help but overhear your conversation, ma'am. Are you interested in a GPS tracker for one of your children? Is that what you were referring to? I might be able to help."

This close, there was something about him that sparked an ember of attraction. His eyes, maybe. Green. Like Satan's. She fluttered her lashes and laid her hand against his chest.

"Please, don't call me ma'am. That makes me feel so old."

His stare dropped to her long red fingernails the minute she touched him and his breath caught. "My name is Lynne and if you could help me, I'd be ever so grateful. Do you think you know what I want?"

She moved her hand to his bicep and down his arm before releasing it, with only the briefest flash that he wasn't as toned as Blake.

He was younger. If she had to guess, maybe by eight or ten years. A broad smile broke out on his face. "I have exactly what you want." His head bobbed. "And I can help you with the tracking device as well."

Young and cocky. She fiddled with the top button on her

blouse, a calculated move to draw his attention back to her breasts. He followed like a lamb to slaughter. "I'm glad to hear that. You look like a man who knows what he's talking about."

At that moment, she could have asked him to stand on his head and he would've gladly complied. "I need one of those thinga majiggies that can attach to a car without the driver knowing about it, but I'm afraid I have no idea what to buy exactly, how it will work or how I'll manage to attach it." She stepped closer and whispered, "This is somewhat of a covert operation, as they say. You know, under covers?"

Phillip's arm snaked around her waist and drew her against his side. "Yes ma'am, I know exactly how to help you."

No, his body was nothing like Blake's but the titillation of that encounter in a public setting balanced out his inferiorities. Blake had already moved out and she was hungry for a man's attentions. They'd walked to the parking lot, climbed into Phillip's truck and she'd straddled him in the passenger seat, riding him like a rodeo bull. The danger of being caught coupled with the thrill of the spontaneity had surprised and delighted her. She'd known then he'd come in handy.

And he had. He bought the device, installed it and tracked Blake for her. She'd explained it was evidence for her divorce case and he hadn't asked another question.

He repeated too often that he was a no-strings kind of guy, enough to annoy her, but she didn't want strings either. At least not with him.

She'd gotten high with him a few times but didn't like the feeling of losing control. He enjoyed smoking weed and became more amiable to doing her bidding when he was wasted, so she allowed it.

He'd been savvy enough to stay on the fringes of her arrest and the subsequent legal proceedings, sitting in the back row in a jacket and tie clutching a yellow piece of paper that gave the appearance he was in the room for his own court appearance.

He'd spotted her in the hallway but hadn't acknowledged her. Clever boy.

He'd found a way to communicate during her ridiculous incarceration in the psychiatric hospital. They hadn't called it that but that's what it was. Eleven days had passed before the envelope arrived, opened of course because there was no privacy in that sterile hell, with only a manager's business card from the auto parts store inside.

They were a good match.

PHILLIP WAITED at the curb while she dutifully bid goodbye to her housemates, gave Fran a peck on the cheek and promised they'd meet for lunch soon. She assured Fran she had the schedule for her continued counseling sessions and would keep the outpatient appointments. Her stomach jumped when she saw him. He remembered her insistence that he always open the car door for her and wait until she was situated to touch the ignition switch. The beard was gone. The fingernails still needed work.

"Whaddaya wanna do first, babe?" She cringed. He hadn't remembered all her directives. "Are ya hungry? It's almost lunchtime. Or do you wanna see the new place?"

She turned her widest smile on him. "I am hungry, but not for food. Let's drive by Argia's school. Maybe she'll be outside for recess and I can see her. Just a glimpse. I miss her so."

His chin tightened at her disregard for him. Men were such babies. She caressed his inner thigh. "One peek at my daughter. And then we can go back to the new apartment and you can make good on all the fantasies you've been whispering to me."

"Gotcha." She suppressed a shudder. He'd need some retraining.

She wouldn't mind a wild romp in the sack with Phillip to

dissipate her jangled nerves, but her daughter was her priority. He called it monkey sex, believing that their coupling was wild and out of control. Little did he know she controlled every minute.

She retrieved the baby doll from her tote and placed it on her lap. First things first. Get the doll into Argia's hands.

To her dismay, Argia wasn't among the children who peppered the playground, or the group organized into a follow-the-leader game. At least it looked like that's what they were playing. It'd been a while since she'd been to the schoolyard. Argia's absence didn't deter her.

"Stay here." She strolled to the chain link fence that corralled the kids and called to the closest child. "Little girl? You. Are you friends with Argia Matthews? Do you know her? This is her dolly. I'm trying to return it to her but I don't see her. Will you give it to her?"

The woman overseeing the children approached. "May I help you?"

A teacher's aide perhaps? She was on the young side. And likely easily manipulated. She raised the doll in the air.

"I do hope so. This doll belongs to Argia Matthews. I wanted to return it but I don't see her outside. Is she in school today?"

The woman reached for the doll. "Argia isn't in this recess group. I'll be happy to take it."

Lynne pressed her hand to her heart. "Thank you so much. If you can't find her, slip it into her backpack. It's blue with the puppy-dog face. She was upset that she forgot it so that will be a sweet surprise."

"And you are?"

Lynne waved and turned. "Thank you so much. Bye now."

12

Blake leaned against his truck's front fender, his arms across his chest, waiting for the explosion of kids rushing to escape the school building. Hell, he remembered his exhilaration at the end of every school day.

Butterflies battled in his belly whenever the last bell of the day rang, knowing that his treasured gift from God would come bounding out the front door and race across the grass to leap into his arms. He cherished that warm feeling when her chestnut curls smothered his face and her arms choked his neck so tight, he could barely breathe. The days he was able to pick up Gia after school were the sweetest.

Ever since the abduction, Gia had been more attached to him than perhaps a six-year-old should be. He didn't mind it at all. It was evident with Noreen as well and a surge of emotion coursed through him every time Noreen embraced his daughter with more love than her mother had ever demonstrated. After what they both survived, Blake didn't care if Gia still hung on them when she was eighteen.

He was happy when she didn't express an interest in riding the bus with her classmates. He hadn't planned on allowing it if she wanted to, and he hated denying her anything. But a daily bus ride was too risky, considering all that had happened.

The attempted burglary at his home the week before remained a question mark. He and Joe had rushed to the house to find the police on scene. They'd discovered the screen from his office window lying in the grass. The paint was scratched and marred at the middle window rail, as if someone with a crowbar had tried to wedge the top and bottom sections apart to slip the lock from its clasp. Near the sill, more scrape marks. He speculated if not a crowbar, a claw hammer might have been used to jiggle the window, likely interfering with the sensor and setting off the burglar alarm. Hard to imagine one person being so dexterous. Also hard to believe the culprit, or culprits, ignored the blue and white octagonal security sign posted in the front yard.

No other windows appeared to have been tampered with. The police searched for footprints, but the concrete patio was clean and the indentations in the grass were useless.

They'd waited for Blake to respond to the security company's call. He knew the cops who'd been dispatched. "Is she out?" one of the officers had asked. There was no need to identify the person he inquired about. The police had united last time in a show of support to aid in finding Gia and Noreen. Joe was correct. They wore different colored uniforms but were brothers just the same.

"No, she's still under supervision. Until Friday. I plan to talk to your chief about that."

"No need, Blake. We'll step up patrols for ya starting tonight. Anything even slightly suspicious, give us a holler."

The officer said no other homes reported attempted break-ins and neighbors he questioned hadn't seen anyone lingering behind Blake's home. In his mind, that was highly suspicious. But he couldn't tell the cops how to do their jobs.

He didn't have to caution Noreen or Brittni, once they were

back at Joe's house. Everyone was extremely cognizant of their surroundings at all times. It had become a habit.

The school bell rang, refocusing his attention on the front door, and he stood straighter, watching for his lightning bolt of love. Her short blue dress flapped around her thighs and her blue puppy backpack swung from her outstretched arms. He knelt and she threw herself against his chest.

"Hi Daddy."

That had to be the sweetest word in the English language. Daddy. "Hey Peanut, how was school today?"

"Miss Linda got mad at me."

He helped her into the truck and tightened the strap on her car seat, sensing his forehead crinkle. "Why did Miss Linda get mad at you?" Gia was a perfect student. None of her teachers ever complained about her.

"She had a baby doll, Daddy, but I didn't want it."

"You mean like a gift she tried to give you and you refused it? Gia, that wasn't nice."

"No. It wasn't a present, Daddy."

He closed the rear door but paused before stepping into the driver's seat and spoke through the open window. "You mean she wanted you to play with a doll from the classroom toy box and you didn't want to? Why would that make her mad?"

Gia focused on her high-top tennis shoes that lit up when she jiggled her feet, bringing the rainbow stripes to life. "It wasn't from the toy box. I didn't want it but she zipped it in my puppy's bag. I hollered, and she got mad."

His brows furrowed. Gia rarely lost her temper over anything. For her to yell at a teacher's aide was out of character. She respected adults. He opened the back door and reached to draw Gia's backpack to him. He spoke as he unzipped it.

"Honey, I don't understand what you're telling me." He removed the doll. "Did Miss Linda give you this doll?"

"No-o-o-o, Daddy, no-o-o. I don't want it." Her feet kicked

the seat in a multi-colored outburst. "I want Mr. Dog and Mr. Fox." She stretched her hands toward him, her fingers wiggling. "Keep them away from her, Daddy. I don't want the doll." Her face flushed red and her bottom lip quivered.

Her beloved stuffed animals traveled to school with her but Gia had strict orders that they had to stay in the backpack the entire day. Her teachers affirmed Gia followed the rules.

He yanked the toys from the bottom of the bag and handed them to her and she buried her face in them. Still confused by her reaction, he quickly dropped the doll back inside and zipped it closed.

"Okay, but if Miss Linda gave you this doll and you don't want it, you can't keep it. You're going to have to give it back and maybe she can give it to another little girl who will be more grateful."

Tears the size of Tic Tac candy pieces rolled down her face. "It's not from Miss Linda."

His heart seized. Gia was genuinely upset and he didn't comprehend the issue. If he didn't understand what was the matter, he couldn't fix it and stop his darling girl's tears.

"I don't understand, Peanut. You said Miss Linda placed the doll in your backpack. If it's not from her, who's it from?"

Gia began to sob. "Mother."

A bucket of ice tossed in his face could not have had a more chilling effect. Noreen had told him about the doll Lynne tried to force on Gia. How the fuck did it end up at her school?

He straightened to peer at the school building over the hood of his truck, but most everyone was gone by now. No matter. He'd call Gia's teacher from home. It was more important to calm Gia.

He removed the backpack from the seat and closed the door. Tossing it into the passenger seat, he climbed inside and started the engine.

"I'm sorry, Peanut. I understand now. It's okay. The doll is up here with me. As soon as we get home, I'll take it away. You don't have to see it again."

Her words were muffled. "Is Weenie home?"

A security blanket for both of them. He might race Gia into the house so he could throw himself into her arms first. "Yes, she is. She's making dinner for us. One of your favorites, I think. And for dessert, how about we all go out for ice cream?"

NOREEN HUNG up the phone just as the garage door went up. She waited to greet the two people who made every day better. The tears on Gia's face puzzled her and she dropped to her knees, her arms outstretched. Gia flew silently into her embrace, trembling, crushing Mr. Dog and Mr. Fox between them. Blake stomped past them and went directly to the dry bar, his face a dark scowl.

He strode back in carrying his bottle of scotch and, when she raised questioning eyes to him, shook his head. She eased Gia backward and wiped the tears with her thumb. Her chubby cheeks were as smooth as silk. "Whatever it is, it's okay now. You're home safe."

Ice cubes dropped into Blake's tumbler.

Gia's chin quivered while her wide eyes stared at her. "Would you like a snack? Dinner won't be for a little while."

Scotch flowed into his glass.

Gia's fingers dug into her upper arms and she declined the offer with a headshake. "How about we change into play clothes and go outside? We can take a walk down to Miss Jenny's and visit her puppy."

He swished the alcohol and the ice clinked. "I'd prefer you both stay inside."

Whatever had happened, it upset Blake as well as Gia. But this wasn't the time to ask, not with Gia about to have a meltdown and Blake ready to detonate. She stood, lifted Gia into her arms and strolled to Blake, wrapping her fingers around his biceps and rolling up on her tiptoes to kiss him. She hated that he was drinking more but his kisses were wet and sweet when he did. His expression was unreadable, except for the color his eyes turned. Darker, like a sky turning black when a storm looms. But with Blake, it meant he wanted her. Those dark gray eyes were the color of desire.

She kissed him a second time. "We'll change clothes and be right out."

Whatever the calamity, it drained Gia. She crawled onto her bed, slipped beneath her blankey and closed her eyes, her animals safely smashed together in her arms. In seconds, her breathing evened and she slept.

Noreen waited a full minute before leaving the bedroom and finding Blake in their bedroom, stepping out of his boots. The tumbler was empty.

"Blake, what happened?"

He spun around, grabbed her arm to draw her into the room and closed the door. He pressed against her with his body and reached for the waistband of her jeans. She wrapped her arms around his neck, the woodsy scent of his cologne pleasantly mixing with the burnt cork aroma on his breath. "Blake, tell me."

"I need to be inside you. You're my rock. Please let me have you." It was a raspy request, heated and imploring. He fumbled with the snap on the front of her pants, undoing it and shoving all garments to the floor. She stepped out of them while he dropped his jeans and boxers and then he leaned forward, pinning her against the door again. The speed of his passion aroused her and when he placed his hands on her bottom and lifted her, she locked her legs around his hips. Blake paused to look at her, his eyes questioning, and she nodded. He slid inside her and moaned, then buried his face in her neck much like Gia had done earlier. They leaned against the door, locked together, motionless, panting, waiting for the hunger they shared to be fed, anticipating the tide of desire that would wash over them and float them away on waves of mutual gratification. It only took minutes.

She silenced her scream when she climaxed by pressing her mouth against his shoulder while Blake exploded with a low groan. Breathless, they clung to each other, Blake supporting her weight with his hands locked beneath her hips, drops of sweat dotting his face. Slowly, his breathing returned to normal.

His face still buried in her neck, he whispered, "Jesus, sweetheart, did I just rape you?"

She ran her fingers through his hair, a little longer these days than the military cut he sported when she first met him. "No, but you are full of surprises. I hope you always want me like that."

Finally, he raised those beautiful gray eyes toward her. His brow was smooth again, his mouth softer. She was a nurse, trained to render aid and help heal. She'd done her job for now.

Blake stepped back and she lowered her feet to the floor. "Let me pour another drink before I tell you what happened today."

How did she heal that?

GIA SAT on Blake's lap on the couch spooning ice cream into her mouth when Noreen emerged from the bedroom after a quick shower. It wasn't like Blake to indulge in treats so close to dinner. His scotch sat out of reach on the kitchen counter. At least he stuck to that promise.

"Dinner should be ready in about thirty-five minutes. I hope that bowl of ice cream hasn't ruined your appetite."

Gia's spoon stopped in mid-air. Two pairs of eyes focused on Noreen.

Blake kissed the top of Gia's head. "It's only a small scoop. Gia had a tough day today, didn't you, Peanut?" His daughter's head moved in an exaggerated nod. "She understands she has to eat her dinner." A second emphatic nod.

"What do you mean?"

Blake smoothed Argia's hair. "Tell Noreen what happened, Peanut."

Gia wiped her mouth on her sleeve. "Mother brought that doll to school. The one I didn't like. She gave it to Miss Linda and Miss Linda put it in my puppy pack. But I yelled at Miss Linda 'cause I didn't want it. But she maked me take it."

Noreen's heart raced. She gulped and automatically corrected Gia. "Made, honey. She made you take it."

"She made me take it," Gia repeated with a nod.

Noreen stared at Blake, disbelief clouding her brain. "How did something like that happen?"

Blake dropped a second kiss atop Gia's head. "I don't know. I called her teacher and left a message. That school has security cameras running. I want to see the video. If the doll came from Lynne, it must mean she's been released. She shouldn't be allowed that close to the school, though. I'm also not happy that Linda forced Gia to take it. That's unacceptable. I understand she's only a school aide but that's of no matter. They're fully aware of our concerns. If Gia's teacher doesn't return my call this evening, I'll go into the school tomorrow when I take her in. I want an explanation."

Gia looked away from the TV screen. "I don't want to go to school tomorrow, Daddy."

Blake's mouth slid into a grin. "I don't want to go to work either but I have to. It's what we do when we're growing up." He brushed her hair with his fingers, rolling it over her shoulders. "And you are growing up just fine. What are you supposed to do if you see your mother or something like that happens again?"

Gia recited her instructions. "I don't holler or get mad. I tell them to call you or Weenie. And I don't leave with anyone but you or Weenie."

"Good girl."

Blake always spoke to Gia like an adult. It was one of the things she loved about him. So many parents she'd seen indulged their children, enabling them to continue bad habits, or bullied them in the belief that ruling with an iron fist worked.

She'd never heard Blake raise his voice to Gia, instead calmly explaining what Gia might have done wrong or shouldn't do and asking that she never do it again. His parenting method worked. The child was an angel.

Their moods when they arrived home suddenly made sense. Noreen had a dozen more questions, but she'd ask Blake later. Right now, her family needed healing.

The tray of healthy homemade chicken nuggets was ready to go into the oven when they arrived home and she slipped it in now. "Chicken nuggies, smashed potatoes, some green beans and a salad for the adults. How does that sound?"

Blake smiled. "Perfect."

Gia wasn't as pleased. "I don't want beans." Usually she ate her vegetables without protest but sometimes, innovation was called for.

"They aren't ordinary beans. These are birthday beans." Her eyes rounded. "You can only eat as many beans as how old you are. We have to count each one before we put it in our mouth. Daddy will have to eat the most."

Gia clapped her hands excitedly and Blake smoothed her hair back. "You'll have to help me count, Peanut."

She nodded happily and Noreen relaxed her shoulders. "And we might have to help Daddy eat them because he'll have a lotta beans." She dragged out the last words and gestured wildly, drawing giggles from Gia.

"And after dinner, ice cream. Daddy said."

"More ice cream?"

"Daddy promised."

Blake shrugged. "I did. A promise is a promise, right Gia?"

Her bottom lip quivered. "What if I go back to school and Mother is there?"

His jaw tightened but his voice remained unruffled. "I'll make sure she's not. What happened today will never happen again. I promise."

13

D ammit. Lynne slammed the laptop shut. The camera device wouldn't work.

Phillip had assured her that a tiny receiver could be concealed in the doll, allowing her to spy on Blake. Especially if Argia dragged it around like she did those disgusting stuffed toys. Of course, Lynne explained that her intention was merely to monitor her child and ensure she was being adequately cared for. Phillip didn't question her motives.

Now, he shrugged. "I guess it's out of range, Babe. It mighta got jarred around and detached. Could be a couple a things. Sorry. I figured it would work. I'm sure the kid is fine."

"Argia is my daughter. Not a kid. A kid is a baby goat." She restrained herself from smacking the befuddled look off his face. She still needed him.

This was the first time he'd come up short with her requests. Thus far, he'd followed her directives to the letter. His friend's apartment was bright, solely because the cheap curtains allowed the light to filter in. The furniture, although used, was somewhat clean. She sat on a towel anyway. It took her two days to sanitize the place. Phillip's buddy lived like a pig. The place reeked of stale smoke, so she kept scented candles burning most of the time.

He'd remembered that her parole officer had to approve her new living accommodations and make surprise inspections, so he stocked the pantry and fridge with healthy food for her. He never touched a vegetable or looked at a piece of fruit.

More importantly, there wasn't a drop of alcohol in the place, despite Phillip's love for beer. He stowed his cases in his trunk.

She'd insisted on decorating Argia's room herself with bright pink walls and frilly curtains. Phillip shrugged when she asked if his friend would mind the refurbishment. Frankly, she didn't care what either of them thought. Blake had often said Argia wasn't a girly-girl but he was wrong. Pink for her was perfect. A projector night-light shown from the corner and cast stars across the ceiling. Even Phillip, when he was high, thought it was magical. Argia was sure to love it.

New outfits filled the closet, dresses with coordinated ruffled socks and shiny patent leather shoes. Not the shabby clothes her father allowed her to wear.

She'd done her best with the allowance the state paid her and the balance in her commissary account. Sifting through Phillip's pockets every night also helped build her money reserve.

Fran had accompanied her parole officer on the first inspection and grinned favorably at the room and the new stuffed animals waiting for Argia's arrival.

But first, Lynne had to convince the courts to allow Argia to spend the night. If only she could control them like she could Phillip.

Today was the first visit outside the confines of Dalton House. She'd be on her best behavior this afternoon, despite the dreadful meeting location. Whoever suggested using the community playground as a neutral site? It wasn't neutral as far as she was concerned. She never remembered Argia playing there.

But Fran cautioned her not to argue with the appointed monitor from child services who viewed the park as a fun, familiar setting. She ran her fingers through Phillip's hair, wishing he'd wash it more often. At least today, he'd make some use of his photography accreditation, despite his aversion to finding a job where he might employ his talents. "Remember, I have my reconciliation meeting this afternoon. I want you there but out of sight. I need a second set of eyes to see who else is there besides that whore-nurse."

Phillip nodded. "Don't worry. I already got my long-distance lens on the camera. You'll have your pictures."

"Keep in mind, I don't want pictures of Argia. I—"

"I know, I know. I got it. I'll shoot everyone who is there."

For shit's sake, he was hiding in the bushes like some convict running from the law. Phillip had never had to do that in his life. Her ex wouldn't be dumb enough to show up today and risk a judge tossing his ass in jail. From the little he knew about the guy, he was smart. Smart enough to set up this meet in a public place so Lynne couldn't snatch the kid and run. He narrowed his eyes to survey the area. Didn't look like anyone was around who might give a crap about Lynne or her kid. He didn't get it.

He snapped a few frames to check his focus. Looked like two people eating lunch at one table, wearing shorts and sunglasses. At another, a woman sat with folders and a brief-case. She wasn't dressed for the park in pants and a long-sleeved jacket. That must be the social worker Lynne told him to look for. He zoomed in and snapped a couple pictures. With the birds chirping and the kids on the soccer field making so much noise, no one heard the click of the camera.

Sweat trickled down the back of his shirt. Lynne had dropped him off a block away from the park entrance. He'd hoofed it to this play area lugging his camera equipment, then crawled into this hiding spot. He could go for a cold beer right about now.

He watched the kid arrive with the nurse. They were holding hands and skipping toward the slide. He couldn't imagine Lynne skipping anywhere, let along playing with her kid in the park like the nurse did. Chasing her. Running from her. That would have been way too much exercise for Lynne who never had a hair out of place or a bead of sweat on her lip. The kid was probably better off with the nurse. She'd sure as hell have more fun with her. Why did Lynne want the kid around anyway? They were better off without her.

Then Lynne appeared on the pathway, tiptoeing her way across the grass. He stifled a laugh. She was definitely out of her element.

Lynne spotted Argia on the sliding board and cringed at the innumerable number of germs and dirt that must cover the thing. This environment was toxic for her daughter. The knees on her jeans were filthy and her hair was a tangled mess. It was so obvious Noreen didn't know how to care for a child. Why couldn't the court see it?

As she stepped gingerly across the grass, trying to keep her heels from poking holes in the dirt, she surveyed the area. No Blake in sight. He wouldn't be stupid enough to violate the court order, but she'd prayed he did. It would end this farce of a custody battle that much sooner. Argia belonged with her.

A young couple sat at a picnic table off to the side. The

man's back was to her. He wore a ball cap backwards and the woman wore sunglasses and a floppy hat. She didn't recognize them. A handful of loud children kicked a ball around on the soccer field, their mothers or nannies or babysitters chatting in nearby chairs and seemingly ignoring their kids. Where the hell was Phillip?

She straightened her back when Argia saw her and shot toward Noreen. The whore-nurse knelt and whispered in her ear. At another table, the court-appointed social service worker rose and waved.

Showtime.

"Hello." Lynne extended her hand. "I'm so sorry to be late. There was more traffic than I expected. I've never been here before."

She placed her designer tote on the table, turned in Argia's direction and clutched her hands to her breasts. "Look at my little girl. Isn't she a beauty?" She waved. "Argia! Argia! Come sit with Mother."

She returned her gaze to the caseworker. "Oh my goodness, I'm so excited I can't stand it. I've missed her so."

Turning back, she felt her jaw tighten when Argia clung to Noreen's hand with both of hers. Noreen bent toward Argia, speaking words she couldn't hear, while they moved at a snail's pace toward the table. When they were about fifteen feet away, Noreen sank to the ground and whispered again. Argia ignored her, first watching the couple at the picnic table, then the group on the soccer field, then returning her attention to the couple. Hmmm. Apparently, she didn't listen to Noreen very well. The child was looking around wildly. That could work in her favor.

Finally, Argia focused on her.

Lynne plastered a smile on her face and opened her arms wide. "Come, Argia. Come sit with me."

As if her shoes were filled with cement, Argia trudged to the table, alternately eyeing the other picnic table, the soccer field, the caseworker, and then her mother. She looked back toward Noreen, who nodded encouragingly, and kept moving forward. Argia walked to the opposite end of the table from where Lynne waited and perched on the edge of the bench seat.

"Hello, my darling. Why so far away? Can I have a hug?"

She gritted her teeth when Argia shook her head hard enough for her pigtails to swing. This wasn't the time for Argia to disobey her or act out. She reached into her tote. "Look what mother brought you. A new coloring book and new crayons. Can we color a picture together?

A second, more forceful negative response. Lynne clamped her lips between her teeth.

The caseworker cleared her throat. "Hello, Argia. My name is Kitty. It's so nice to meet you. I'll be coming along with your mom when she meets you so you'll get used to seeing me. Just pretend I'm not here. Would you like to color in your new book?"

Argia's chin quivered. She shook her head a third time. She shouldn't be allowed to disrespect adults. Lynne pivoted in search of Noreen. She'd moved to a picnic table directly in Argia's line of sight and sat on top of it, her feet on the bench seat, watching them, a grim look on her face. The woman didn't know better than to abuse public property. She had no ethics. After all, she'd come between her and Blake in her capacity as Argia's nurse, hadn't she?

Seeing the caseworker jot in a notebook, Lynne released an exasperated breath. "This isn't going to work, Kitty. With that woman hovering over there like a bat, I can't connect with my daughter. Why in the world can't she simply come to my place? You'll be there."

"No!" Argia yelled so loud the couple at the table turned to look.

Goodness, her child had lost all her manners. "Argia, shame on you. It's not polite to yell. Don't make a spectacle."

Glancing back, Noreen no longer sat on the table but stood several feet away from it, closer to them. She glared at Lynne, her arms locked across her chest.

Argia began swinging her foot into the table support, banging it to make a low thud. This visit wasn't going at all as she'd planned. Lynne pinched the bridge of her nose and silently counted to five.

"All right, Argia, I understand. You haven't seen my new apartment yet so it's perfectly reasonable that you wouldn't want to go there." She said that more for Kitty's sake than her daughter's. A child should listen to her parents' commands, not defy them. Blake had let all discipline disappear while she'd been in his care.

"For today, let's just sit here and talk. Would that be okay?" She threw her leg over the bench seat and sat at the table. Her slacks would be filthy after sitting here. She'd have to throw them away. But aside from straightening her back and continually pounding her foot against the table, Argia remained sitting. That was progress, wasn't it? And worth a pair of pants.

"Tell me about your school. Do you like your teacher? Do you have a lot of friends?"

Argia's gaze lowered to the tabletop but she nodded.

"Oh, I'm glad. What's your favorite part of class? Your teacher said it was coloring. That's why I bought you the new book and crayons." She moved the items closer to Argia. "Here, Argia, see what picture you want to draw first."

Lynne squared her shoulders and directed her comment to Kitty. "I'm in regular contact with Argia's school. It's important for a parent to monitor their child's progress, don't you think?"

The truth was, she had no idea who was Argia's teacher. But Kitty didn't need to know that, and she must be buying her story. She jotted more notes in a composition notebook.

Lynne tilted her head toward her daughter. "Argia, it dawns on me that no one ever asked you where you'd like to meet when we get together. We've been separated so long, we must learn to know each other again. But someone else has always decided where we meet. Do you have someplace you'd like us to go together? Maybe for ice cream?"

The dairy would make Argia sick but Lynne wasn't making headway like this. At this rate, Argia would be driving to these mother-daughter reconciliation sessions. And she couldn't tolerate much more of this park.

Bugs buzzed her ears, her armpits were sticky and there were too many distractions. Argia kept looking all around her, fascinated by the young couple at the other table, interested in the kids kicking the ball, focusing on everything except her mother.

"Argia, I asked you a question. I know you heard me. It's impolite not to answer. Is there some place you'd like to go?"

Those dark brown eyes stared at her and she folded her hands in front of her to keep from slapping that face.

"I want to go home to Daddy."

She could have throttled the girl, but this wasn't the time to reprimand her. A few days of throwing up would make her appreciate her mother and how much she cared for her. But first, she had to get her alone.

"Really, Argia—"

"I want to go home!" She screamed so loud, the couple at the table both rose to their feet and glared. At the soccer field, another woman stood, dropped her hands on her hips and stared. How humiliating. She should mind her own business. Noreen approached as well.

"Kitty, there's been a misunderstanding. I—"

Argia pounded her fists on the table and screamed, "I want my Daddy. I want to go home."

Noreen called her name and Argia jumped from the bench and raced to her open arms. Scooping her up, Noreen stepped to their table and leveled her gaze on Kitty. "This meeting is over." She pivoted and strode away without waiting for a response.

"How dare she!" Lynne's anger erupted. "You see her disregard for the courts?" She stretched out her arm and pointed toward Noreen's back. "She's kidnapping my daughter. This is what I have to put up with. I hope you're writing all this down. I want some justice."

Kitty closed her book and stood. "The relationship with your daughter seems tenuous at best, Mrs. Matthews. I question if there is a connection at all. It certainly doesn't appear so to me. I—"

A stabbing pain struck behind Lynne's eyes. "You can't make that judgment based on today. I'll never make any headway with my daughter as long as that, that" she flung her arm in the direction Noreen had walked, "that woman is nearby. She's turned my daughter against me." She stomped her heel into the ground. "I won't allow you—"

Kitty halted the outburst like a cop stopping traffic. "I suggest you stop right there, Mrs. Matthews, before you say something you'll regret. I've reviewed all the tapes from the visits you had with Argia at the transitional living home and I see no affection at all between you two. I'm certified in child behavior and I know fear when I see it. I'm going—"

Her outrage boiled over like hot lava. "Don't tell me he got to you too. How much did he pay you? You don't know a thing about Argia. How could you—"

Kitty's eyes widened. "Again, Mrs. Matthews, I caution you about the words you spew. I'm going to recommend that the court speak with your daughter without any parent in the room. I—"

Lynne spat at her. "She's only six years old. What the hell can she tell the court? She doesn't know what's best for her."

Kitty turned to walk away. "I'll forward a copy of my report to your parole officer. Have a good day."

Lynne breathed so heavily, the buttons on her shirt strained tight. She stood beside the picnic table speechless. The urge to run after the caseworker and pummel her wrestled with the image she needed to portray to whoever might be watching. The couple at the other table were seated again, both staring at their phones. The woman at the soccer field remained standing but appeared to be ignoring her. She spun in a three-hundred-and-sixty-degree circle. Where the hell was Phillip?

14

N oreen sensed her eyebrows knit while she assisted
Gia with her seatbelt. No tears. Normally, a meeting
with Lynne resulted in a flood of water and a sullen
mood for hours afterward.

Gia's cheeks were strawberry red, but her eyes were dry. Her
lips were squished together in a pout and her hands fisted so
tight, her pudgy knuckles were white.

"Are you okay, sweetheart?"

"I wanna go home."

"Yes ma'am. Me too."

Noreen buckled her seatbelt and glanced in the rearview
mirror. Lynne still stood at the table, looking around like a wild
woman, her hands in the air and her hair flying. Over her left
shoulder, Joe and Brittni remained at the picnic table. Likely
they'd wait for Lynne to leave.

Down on the soccer field, Rob's girlfriend smiled in her
direction.

The edges of her mouth sneaked up. There wasn't one
second when she felt that she or Gia were in danger. Blake

wouldn't have it any other way. She cruised to the park entrance and allowed a full-blown grin.

"Gia, honey, look out the window. Your Dad and Uncle Rob are in this car. They're going to follow us home. Do you see them?"

Gia didn't respond. Her face was buried in Mr. Fox and Mr. Dog.

At the first stoplight, Noreen looked over her shoulder to the back seat. "Hey! Talk to me. Are you okay?"

Still no tears when Gia lifted her face. "We're gonna run away, Weenie. I love Daddy and I love you. But we have to run away to get away from Mother."

Her heart jerked at the same time the driver behind them honked. Blake always spoke to Gia like an adult and never discredited her fears or fantasies. Which one was this?

"Who is going to run away, honey? Why?"

"Me and Mr. Fox and Mr. Dog. We have to."

Noreen stifled a sob. "Running away is a big decision. You have to be a big girl to run away and I know you are but still, running away is hard to do. Have you thought about this for a long time?"

In the mirror, tear-filled eyes met her gaze. Argia shook her head.

"So, it's just something you decided today? Is it because of the meeting with your mother because once I tell your Dad about it, I bet there will be no more meetings like this. Is that the reason?"

Argia remained silent.

"Running away isn't easy, you know. It takes some strategy. Do you know what that is?"

Gia didn't.

"Well, have you thought about where you might go? You can't just walk out the door without knowing where to go. If you're going to run away, you need a plan."

Gia's eyes widened.

"I think we should all talk about this tonight, you, me and your Dad. You wouldn't run away without telling him, would you? That would break his heart. You don't want to hurt him, do you?"

Gia's bottom lip protruded, and her chin quivered. "I don't want to run away, but I have to."

"Why do you think you have to do that, Gia?"

"Daddy is going to get in trouble."

"Why do you think that?"

"He will hurt Mother."

The lump in her throat was too big to swallow. Out of the mouths of babes. On the tip of her tongue sat the response, 'if he doesn't, I will. And there's a long list of folks behind me with the same idea.' But that wasn't the correct reply to allay Gia's fears.

"That might happen if you run away, Gia, because your Dad would be terrified, and he could lash out at your mom. He might think she took you like last time. If you don't run away, you will keep him from doing that. Remember how he listened to you in the hospital? He wanted to hurt you mom then and you stopped him."

"Daddy's different now."

"What do you mean? How is he different?"

"He's madder."

Well, she couldn't argue with that.

She turned off the ignition in the driveway. Behind her car, Blake exited Rob's truck and approached Gia's side of the car. He yanked the door open and reached inside to unbuckle his daughter. That's when the dam broke.

Gia crushed Blake's neck in an embrace and mumbled into his neck. "Don't be mad at me, Daddy. I don't want to run away. I don't want to hurt your heart."

Over Gia's shoulder, Blake looked at her with questioning

eyes and her vision blurred through her own tears.

She motioned for them to walk inside just as Joe and Brittni drove into the driveway.

Blake stood in the middle of the living room, Gia clinging to him like skin, mumbling. "Peanut, what is it? My heart is okay. Honey, what's the matter?"

Noreen motioned for Joe and Brittni to sit, poured wine for her and Brittni and handed Joe a cold beer. She perched on the edge of the loveseat and spoke to Gia's back.

"We can talk about this, honey. Do you want to tell your Daddy what you think you have to do or do you want me to? I think you'll feel better if we discuss it and make a plan. Uncle Joey and Miss Brittni might be able to help."

Curiosity colored Blake's face. His eyebrows rose and his hands stretched out palms up. He sank to the floor and nudged his daughter away from his shoulder, positioning her between his crossed legs. "This is how we sit for a powwow. What's going on Peanut? What can we help you plan?"

His reaction to Gia's comment that she had to run away fractured Noreen's heart. Blake's eyes widened, his head jerked backward, and his voice caught.

"Run away? Why? Aren't you happy here? My God, Gia, I love you so much. What's the matter? Why would you want to leave me?"

He failed to control his quivering chin as Gia stuttered her reason before throwing herself into his chest and sobbing her despair. Noreen pressed her fist to her mouth and Joe muttered a curse. When a tear rolled from the corner of Blake's eye, she muffled her own sob.

Brittni dropped to her knees and crawled to Blake and Gia. She tapped Gia on the shoulder. "Hey, Gia. Look at me. Can I say something?"

Blake gently rocked Gia while she turned her tear-streaked face toward Brittni who sat back on her haunches. "We're buddies, right? Bestest friends." Gia's bottom lip protruded forward, quivering.

"And bestest friends help each other with everything, right?" Gia offered an affirmative nod.

Brittni nodded as well. "Okay, good. So here's what I think. I understand how you feel, but don't run away right now. Let's give Noreen and your Dad a little time to work things out so you can stay with them forever. Then if they can't figure that out and you still want to run away, I'll help you. Maybe I'll even come with you so it's not so scary."

Gia's swollen eyes lifted to peer at Brittni. "You will?"

Brittni smiled." Of course I will. That's what bestest friends do."

"And you'll tell Daddy so his heart doesn't hurt?"

"Yes, and we'll tell Joey too so his heart isn't hurt."

"Do you promise you'll run away with me?"

"If you think that's what you have to do, I promise. Pinkie swear." She extended her upraised finger toward Gia, who giggled and wrapped her small finger around it.

Blake breathed an audible sigh of relief and swiped at his cheek. He dropped a kiss on the top of Gia's head. "I'm glad that's settled, at least for now. It's been a trying day for all of us, Peanut. How about me and you go take a nap?" Gia agreed and Blake carried her to her room.

When he returned, Noreen and Brittni huddled around Joe's phone, watching as he slid his thumb sideways to advance the photos on the screen.

Blake reached for Brittni and drew her into a hug. "How can I thank you?"

She waved off his words. He turned and wrapped his arms around Noreen's waist, kissed the side of her neck and peered over her shoulder at Joe's phone.

"Who's that?"

Joe shrugged. "Lynne had a friend with her at the park this

afternoon. These aren't the best images. He wore a ball cap pulled low. And I could only take side shots from my vantage point without being conspicuous." Blake stepped away from her and took the phone.

The kid looked young. Not what he'd call Lynne's type. "I've never seen him before. That's a pretty expensive camera hanging around his neck. Could she have hired a private investigator? How did she afford one?"

They were stumped. He leveled his gaze on Noreen. "I don't need to remind you—"

Noreen mimicked him, tilting her head from side to side. "...to be extra careful and keep my eyes open for this man. I know, Blake. We all do." Her wide smile and shuffle into his arms broke the tension of the moment and he grinned.

"I was only going to remind you that I love you."

15

A nother Unknown Caller. Noreen diligently noted the time and date in the small notebook she kept in her purse. This was a deviation. The calls never came when she was at the hospital. She didn't keep her personal phone on her and only checked it this time when it rang because she was digging in her purse for the salad recipe Kelly wanted.

The hairs on the back of her neck pinched while she stared at the capital letters on the screen.

There was something familiar about this number. She almost recognized it. Not for sure, but the sequence of digits was repetitive. It probably was a random solicitor ignoring the government's Do Not Call restrictions. Or a robot call. Everyone was complaining more and more about them. However, this particular robot had dialed in before. She was certain. Just for the heck of it, she jotted down the number beside the time and date.

These calls elevated her internal warning bells to high alert, but she couldn't explain why. Except that they were becoming more frequent. Ominous silence prevailed on the other end, like a dangerous cavern into which she might fall, whenever she relented and answered. It would've been better if she heard heavy breathing. At least then, she could write it off as a pervert. Instead, the silence left her with an uneasy feeling, and she rejected each call with a growing sense of foreboding.

Standing at the other end of the horseshoe, Kelly slammed her phone down. "I swear there's a curse hanging over my head. First the television goes down the tank. Then the washing machine quits with a full load of heavy, wet towels. And now the mechanic says my car needs some hi-tech computer part that must be ordered. What next could go wrong?"

Noreen smiled at her friend. "They say bad luck comes in threes so maybe you're finished now. I didn't know you were having car trouble. When did that happen?"

"When I was driving home after our last shift. All these lights started blinking on the dashboard and some damn bell kept dinging. I dropped it off this morning on the way in and jumped on the bus. But that ain't gonna get me home or back here tomorrow."

"Don't worry about that. I'll run you home. And I can pick you up on the way in tomorrow. And if you're still without a ride when we end shift, you can drop me off and take my car home. Blake is off after tomorrow and I can use his truck."

"Girl, I can't put you out like that."

"You're not putting me out. End of discussion."

Today had been an easy day on the pediatric surgical floor with only three patients to monitor. They'd had time for her to confide in Kelly about the baby doll incident, the visitation with Lynne in the halfway house, and the disastrous meeting at the park. Both agreed that Brittni had hit on the right solution for Gia's idea to run away by supporting it rather than telling her no. In Gia's mind, Brittni was an ally, not an adult. That reassured her and Blake.

Kelly applauded Blake's idea to have Brittni and Joe at the

park as well as Rob's girlfriend, who brought her niece to play with the children on the soccer field.

"I'll be happy to spy on the next meeting. That woman doesn't know my face."

Noreen's shoulders sagged. "Unfortunately, the next meeting is a one-on-one with Gia and the judge. I'm not sure how that will go."

"What are you worried about? Argia is smart and capable of telling the judge she wants to live with her father."

"Yes, but if the idea of running away comes up, that could work against Blake."

Kelly shook her head. "The law just doesn't seem fair, sometimes. Move my name to the top of that available guardian list. I won't let that woman get her hands on your sweet girl. She'd have to kill me first. And believe me, that wouldn't happen."

They were walking to the car and Noreen frowned. "We already know she's capable of that. Killing, I mean. Blake is as worried as I am, especially after what happened at the school. She shouldn't have been allowed that close to Gia or any of the children. We want to hire private security for Argia when she's in school."

They snapped their seatbelts. "I don't blame you. Is that possible?"

Noreen shrugged. "He spoke to the school administrators and they say it would create an intrusion in the classroom. The school insists they can keep an eye on her. They might consider guards outside the building if they are discreet, but they didn't confirm that. Her teacher is dedicated to Gia so, theoretically, Gia is safe when she's in the classroom. But she was ill the day Lynne somehow delivered the baby doll so that's a perfect example that validates the request for extraordinary measures. What if another student has an emergency and the teacher is called away? What if Lynne pulls the fire alarm to create pandemonium or a water pipe breaks and floods the halls, causing a commotion? There are too many unknowns to rely on her teacher or anyone in that school to monitor Argia when they are responsible for a whole building of children. I don't want to take that chance. Neither does Blake. We just haven't come up with a viable plan."

She edged her car onto the parkway, happy to merge smoothly into her lane, and checked her rearview mirror. "Well Kell, your luck must be changing. Look, there's barely any traffic this morning." Despite the two open lanes to her left, a black boxy-looking vehicle zoomed up behind them. Noreen gripped the steering wheel and applied pressure to the gas pedal, although she was already moving at sixty-five miles per hour. Still, the black square edged closer.

"What the hell?"

"What's the matter?"

"This creep is riding my bumper." The windows were tinted black. She couldn't make out a driver or passenger.

Kelly rotated to see behind them just as the driver hit the back of the car, throwing her forward to the dashboard. Noreen grasped the wheel tighter to steer but the force of a second harder impact caused her to veer wildly to the right and then left.

"Get off the road!" Kelly yelled.

She didn't have time. The phantom driver rammed her a third time and she lost control, crashed into the guardrail, careened off it, and sideswiped a car in the lane next to her, sending it zigzagging uncontrollably to the right. Her car rebounded back into the guardrail, hurtled through it, and plummeted down an embankment. She screamed. Kelly screamed. They bounced down the hill through a buffer of trees and shrubs and came to a stop when the car spun in a circle and the driver's door embedded into a tree.

The airbags deployed with the deafening sound of a gunshot.

"Oh my God, Kelly, are you all right?" Blood flowed from Kelly's nose and oozed from a gash on her head but she nodded, using her hands in a swimming motion to shove the safety fabric off her lap. Noreen wiped her own nose to discover blood, and gingerly touched her forehead over her burning left eye. It was wet and gooey. Sweat or blood rolled down the side of her face.

A woman's voice filled the car's interior. "Miss Jensen? This is your navigation operator. We've detected that you've had an accident. We've notified the police. Help is on the way. Miss Jensen? Are you injured? Can you respond?"

PHILLIP SLAMMED ON HIS BRAKES. Holy shit! She swerved right off the road. Jesus, he didn't mean for that to happen. He only tapped her bumper. It wasn't that hard of a hit. He clutched the steering wheel, his lungs pounding against his ribs, and stared into the rearview mirror. Nothing but the mangled guardrail with a fresh swipe of blue paint across it. Should he go check on her? What if she was dead? What if someone saw him?

Playing Lynne's little 'Game of Fear' had been fun up until now. This trip was only supposed to scare the nurse. "Let her know it's going to be a bumpy ride unless she gets out of my daughter's life," Lynne had said. He didn't see the harm in tailing the nurse, maybe crowding her a little. Just a friendly game of chicken.

He pressed his fists into his eyeballs. If he hadn't gotten high first, he might not have been so careless. But man, it was a thrill just stepping behind the wheel of his buddy's Humvee. He was the fucking king of the road in this vehicle. One tap on the gas pedal and the thing shot forward like a missile. The velocity surprised him. He should get out and check if there was any damage. He doubted it. Not with that cowcatcher on the front.

He slammed the steering wheel. She wasn't supposed to crash like that. Just get scared enough to pull over and stop. Then he could whiz by. Maybe give her the finger. She wouldn't see it through the tinted windows, but he'd enjoy it.

He rolled down the window and wiped the sweat off his forehead with his sleeve.

What if she was dead? Maybe he could walk to the edge where she went over the embankment and see her. Maybe he'd see the nurse standing up just fine beside her wrecked car. What if she needed help? If he reported the accident, they could trace the call. What if someone saw him along the edge of the road? Fuck. This whole scheme of Lynne's was getting too crazy for him.

Sirens caught his attention. Who called the police? Did someone see him? Well, if help was on the way, he didn't need to stick around. He pressed the ignition start button. Someone would find her.

~

"Miss Jensen? This is your navigation operator. Can you hear me? Are you able to respond?"

Noreen burst into tears. "Yes, yes, I can hear you. Thank you." Kelly lowered her head between her knees and vomited.

"Someone ran us off the road. We need an ambulance."

"We've notified all emergency services. I'll stay on the line with you until help arrives. Are you alone?"

She stretched to touch Kelly's shoulder and the motion caused everything in her line of sight to waver. She shut her eyes. "No, my friend is with me." Kelly sat up and gasped.

"Lay your head back, Noreen, you have a gouge across your

eye spouting blood like a fountain." She squeezed Noreen's hand.

The navigation woman spoke again. "Don't move until help arrives, Miss Jensen. They're close. They should be there momentarily."

Sirens blared in the distance. The landscape visible through the spider-webbed windshield began to jiggle, as if the ground beneath it shook. The odor of Kelly's vomit filled the car and her stomach revolted. Still pressed against her seat by her locked seatbelt and unable to move, she expelled her morning breakfast down the front of her clothes.

"It's okay, girl, we seen puke before. At least we're alive." Kelly opened the passenger door for air and the sirens abruptly stopped. Thank God.

In seconds, rescuers shouted orders and branches crunched under heavy, booted feet. Hearing Joe's voice, Noreen started to cry again.

"Jesus. Noreen? Kelly? Don't move until we can assess your injuries."

Kelly unsnapped her seatbelt. "Get me outta here, Joey, or I'm gonna retch again."

"Take it easy. You know the drill. Let me do my thing."

Noreen gulped for air. Their voices were faint, as if they spoke from a tunnel off in the distance. Her vision blurred. Her chest pounded. She couldn't catch her breath. Her hand moved through the air as if detached from her body, waving wildly. Kelly grabbed it and spoke to her.

"Noreen?" Her name echoed in her ears. Kelly's mouth moved in slow motion. "Noreen? C'mon, girl, stay with me." But it sounded like staaayyyy wiiiittthh meeee.

She was back in that dark hole beneath the porch of Blake's former home. Locked in the room with Gia in total darkness. In agonizing pain from her broken leg. The fumes from the oil lamp Lynne Matthews used to set the room on fire clogged her nasal passages. Flames were all around her and she was crawling for her life. She waved her hands frantically in the air to ward them off.

The odor was real. The fumes right here. Right now. She was back in the cellar. Burning to death. "No, no fire. Please. Help me. Don't let me burn. Someone help me." The pitch of her voice rose. "No, no, no. No flames. No fire."

Joe hovered over her. "Noreen, calm down. It's okay. We're right here."

Her head rolled from side to side. Why couldn't she see? "Don't let me burn. Please don't let me burn."

Joe's gloved hand gripped both of hers together. "Listen to me. You're okay. You smell gas and oil that leaked from the engine. But there's no fire. Do you hear me? You're not in a fire. We're going to get you out of here but it will take a couple minutes. You need to relax."

Gia. Where was Gia? "Gia! Keep Gia safe. Where's Gia?"

"Noreen, look at me." A bundle of gauze pressed against her eyes. "Let's stanch this bleeding." He applied pressure to her forehead. "Is that better?" No, everything was blurred.

"Gia is fine. You're fine. I'm here and Blake is on his way. You're hyperventilating and starting to panic. You have to calm down."

He forced her to extend her arms. "Place your hands on the steering wheel. Concentrate on holding onto that. That's right. Now look at me. Look at me. Do you see me? Do you see Joe?"

Her vision was clearing. Her machine-gun breaths slowing down. His face came into focus. More tears rolled out of the corners of her eyes and down her cheeks. "Joey?"

He smiled. "Yes, ma'am." He covered her left eye with a fresh bandage. "You've got a hell of a gash over your eye. Let's keep it closed and covered while we work to get you out of here. Let me wrap it." He rolled the gauze around her head.

She grabbed his wrist, feeling anxious again. "How're you going to get me out? I'm trapped."

"Aw, Noreen, this is what we train for. This is a piece of cake, hon. You with me?"

Her heart was zooming like a freight train, but she nodded.

"Good girl. Do you have any neck pain?"

She shook her head. "What about your back? Your legs? Can you feel your legs? Can you move your feet?"

She tried. The airbag lay heavy on her lap. She couldn't move.

"I...I can't move my legs." Fear etched her voice. Dear God, she was paralyzed.

"It's all right. Let me see." Joe leaned over and ran his hands along her thighs. "This car crunched like an accordion. Can you feel this?" He squeezed her knee.

Relief relaxed her. "Yes."

He squeezed again. "Which knee?"

The tension in her shoulders dissipated. "Right." From somewhere behind her, a generator purred into action. Joe hovered with a tarp spread wide.

"Noreen, the only way to get you out of here is straight up. We're going to pop the roof off the car, which means we have to cut the four posts. It'll be fast but I don't want any pieces flying at you. I'm going to cover you with this tarp, okay?"

Panic swept over her as he lowered the tarp, erasing every inch of daylight.

"No!" She screamed and reached upward to block the blackness. "No. Don't cover me. Don't leave me in the dark."

"Shit. I forgot. Somebody hand me a flashlight."

"Joe, I..."

"It's okay. We can do this together. Just stay calm. Lewey is here so don't make me look bad." He switched on a flashlight and drew the tarp over both of them, stretching to extend coverage over her shoulder. "There. See? Just like camping in a tent. Let me get this." From somewhere, he produced a blade and sheared the seatbelt. The pressure across her chest released.

High-powered cutters whirred into motion and metal squealed and cracked. His face was inches from hers. "Tell me how you feel. Any pain at all? Did your head hit the windshield? Can you wiggle your toes?"

"No, I didn't hit the windshield. Yes, I feel my toes moving. Nothing feels broken. Guess that steel rod in my left leg came in handy. It's a good thing. I'm not ready for another round of crutches."

Joe grinned and lifted the tarp. She stared at the trees and the bright cloudless sky. Her four-door sedan was suddenly a convertible. Then a responder she didn't recognize was in front of her, cranking back the steering wheel and using a tool to raise the dashboard. The weight lifted off her legs.

She turned her head to find Blake but Joe was back, standing over her, straddling the seats, blocking her view. "That better? Can you move your legs now?"

She did and smiled.

"That's great. We're going to help you crawl out of here. Ready?"

Two men climbed into the back seat and braced her when Joe reclined the seat. The three of them lifted her upward while she pushed with her legs, onto the seat cushion, over the console and onto the ground. Her knees buckled but more hands and arms extended toward her. No one let her fall. These men never would.

"Let's get the stretcher, gentlemen, just to be safe." Blake's deep voice washed over her like warm massage oil and then his beautiful gray eyes were staring down at her. He winked and she felt immensely better. "I've been thinking about buying you a new car anyway."

"Blake, where's Gia?"

"Mom's with her. She's fine."

She swiveled her head to look around. "Kelly? What about Kelly? Is she all right?'

Joe grabbed her upper arms. "She's already on the way to the hospital, just as a precaution. How about you sit on this."

"I don't need a stretcher. I'm fine."

Blake reached for her. "Yep, nurses and doctors make the worst patients. That's a hell of an embankment we have to climb. Do me a favor and let us transport you."

Before she could argue, she was safely belted on a cot and six men trudged up the hillside. They weren't even out of breath when they reached the top.

She refused an oxygen hose. This hadn't been an accident. Someone deliberately ran them off the road. She was certain of it. Someone tried to kill them. She needed to tell him that. "Blake, that other car—"

Joe's face appeared again. "Noreen, your numbers are spiking again. Please stay calm. We're going to load you into the ambulance now. There'll be plenty of time to talk at the hospital."

She was jarred and jostled and locked into place. Doors slammed and the ambulance jerked into motion. Blake. Where was he?

As if reading her thoughts, Blake gripped her ankle. "I'm right here, sweetheart. Relax and listen to Joey."

THIS WAS the worst déjà vu moment of his life, sitting in an ambulance at Noreen's feet, watching Joe and Rob tend to her, silently praying that she'd be okay. Just like last year when her burned, lifeless body lay on the stretcher and he and Gia crouched at her ankles praying that she'd live. At least today, she was conscious, but had she suffered internal injuries they were unaware of? Was she bleeding out even now and in seconds be snatched out of his life? Sure, she was walking and talking but he'd seen patients act the same one minute and keel over the next.

"How's she sound, Joe?"

He wrapped the stethoscope around his neck and nodded. "As far as I can tell, all we're dealing with are bumps and bruises. She still says nothing hurts. Of course, they'll know more at the hospital." Noreen's chest rose and fell with her sigh.

WHILE HE WAITED outside the examining room, Blake called his mother. She'd gotten Gia off to school, since both he and Noreen were working, and now he wanted her in the cafeteria with Gia at lunchtime. Gia would delight in having Grammy there for lunch. And he'd feel better. This accident didn't feel right. Kelly's account was full of holes.

The doctors examined her and released her with a caution to take it easy the next few days. Most of the impact had occurred on the driver's side. He hugged Kelly for a good thirty seconds before asking how she felt. She was as feisty as ever.

"Ain't no little car accident gonna take us out. Praise the Lord, he was riding with us today."

"What happened?"

"I don't know for sure. My mouth was running like it always does and then Noreen said someone was riding her tail and I turned to look and bam! He was smacking us in the rear."

"Did you see the driver? Did you get a good look at the vehicle?"

"No, it all happened too fast. All I can tell you is that it was a black, big-ass boxy car, almost like a Humvee. What I am sure of is that it wasn't an accident. We were deliberately shoved off the road."

The police officer standing beside them taking notes asked if Kelly would file a complaint. "You're damn right I will."

"Do you know of anyone who would want to hurt you or Miss Jensen?" For the officer, it was a routine question. Kelly's eyes bore holes into Blake, waiting for him to offer up the woman they both suspected. But how could he blame Lynne without proof? He gave Kelly an imperceptible nod and she returned her attention to the cop.

"No one comes to mind right away, officer. Let me think about it."

Like Kelly, Noreen was released with contusions, bruises, and butterfly stitches over her eye, and advised to do as little as possible. The doctors ordered Blake to follow concussion protocol just as a precaution, monitoring Noreen's balance and cognitive functions, watching for signs of impairment and urging her to rest. She insisted she was fine.

Both women would likely be sore the next few days. Blake had notified the hospital about the accident and their next shift that night was covered. Neither woman agreed to take a couple days off to recuperate and argued they'd be fine for work the following night. They compromised with a "let's see how we feel" attitude.

Blake hugged Kelly outside her home. "Make sure you rest. If you feel off in any way, call an ambulance first, and then call me. Think about changing your mind about working tomorrow night. If you still want to go in, I'll pick you up at six tomorrow evening and take you in, probably with Noreen. You two are both pretty stubborn. I hope you both reconsider and take at least one more shift to recover.

"I'm off so I'll take Gia to school and then come for you both in the morning. Breakfast will be on me. Take some aspirin when you get inside and please, call me if anything spooks you or doesn't seem right."

"I can't impose like that. I'll see if I can get a ride from my

Adam or I'll take the bus. It's not a big deal. You should worry about Noreen and your sweet Gia and take care of them."

Noreen had described Kelly as her most loyal friend when she'd first introduced them. He understood why.

"Yes, ma'am. I will. But I'm also looking out for you. This isn't your boyfriend's concern and it shouldn't be yours either. Don't fight me on this or the bright red fire engine will be your transport tomorrow night and your neighbors will have a field day speculating about that. We'll pick you up at six. Now go inside and rest."

She nodded and kissed his cheek. "I'll be fine. You make sure you keep your eyes open too. See you tomorrow."

Once they were alone, driving home, Noreen closed her eyes and laid her head on the headrest. "Tell me what you're thinking," she whispered.

The corners of his mouth edged downward. "I should have killed her."

16

L ynne fanned the photos out to inspect the array. The thrill of such close-up camera shots of her daughter competed with a festering fury over the context of the pictures.

Argia laughing on the playground with Blake's whore-nurse. Argia racing across the grass to Blake's outstretched arms. The three of them smiling around a high, round table eating ice cream. How had Phillip gotten *that* picture? Dammit, Argia was lactose intolerant. What the hell was the matter with her father? Lynne separated that one from the pile. It could be useful in the case she was building against Blake to show he was an unfit father.

She moved to the pile of photos taken last week at the park. They didn't show much. From his vantage point in the trees, Phillip's lens captured mostly pictures of Noreen, laughing with Argia before her arrival. The panoramic view only included the couple at the picnic table. For a minute, there seemed to be something familiar about the man. Probably just her attraction to broad shoulders and a slim waist like Blake's. Her attempts to get Phillip to exercise had fallen on deaf ears.

She studied a newspaper clipping that was part of the surveillance package Phillip handed her that morning. Blake had saved someone else's life and was receiving a merit award. He didn't even look at the camera, instead smiling and staring down at his whore-girlfriend who returned his gaze as if no one else was in the room. How inconsiderate.

She lifted the photos of Noreen Jensen and hissed like an agitated viper. Noreen rushing from the hospital to her car, her head buried below her coat collar to minimize the damage from the pelting rain. Noreen strolling through the grocery store. Lynne positioned a magnifying glass over the contents of her shopping cart. Oh my God, if that's what she was feeding Argia, she was killing her. She spied a family-size box of popcorn shrimp, a large bag of chicken nuggets and, for Pete's sake, candy bars.

Leaning against the kitchen sink, Phillip belched. "Is that enough or do you want more?"

She couldn't bear seeing any more pictures of Argia in that woman's clutches. "Just of the woman." She didn't dare speak Noreen's name. "Every chain has a weak link. She's it, I think."

Phillip shrugged. "I disagree. Since the car accident, she's rarely by herself. The only time I see her walking alone is in that parking lot because it's secured by a guard. They relocated her spot closer to the guard station. She must signal him somehow because he has eyes on her the minute she leaves the building. Beyond that, there's always someone with her, except when she runs into the grocery store on the way home in the mornings. I think you should look closer at the babysitter. I think she's the link to break."

She slammed her open palm on the table. "Dammit, Phillip, the babysitter isn't the issue. Blake's whore is."

He shrugged. "I get that. But just like you used the kid to lure the nurse before, you can use the babysitter. She could, I don't know, have an accident or something and the Jensen woman would have to change up her schedule to watch the kid or something. I don't know exactly but I think the babysitter is your window of opportunity."

"It's not the babysitter who needs to have a fatal accident, you dope, it's that bitch who usurped my position with Argia." She couldn't stand to think her name let alone speak it.

Phillip winced and she immediately regretted the insult. She needed him for more than just a place to stay and a romp in the hay. He was the unseen blip on Blake's radar. Her surprise secret weapon. So what if the police caught him and he spent the rest of his life in jail? As long as he eliminated Noreen Jensen before that, she was fine with the outcome. But she couldn't afford to alienate him yet.

She rose from the table and strolled to him, smoothing her blouse so his eyes would focus on her hands. "Forgive me." She cupped his face. "You know I lose my sanity when I think about that woman. That's why I need you." She kissed his mouth, ignoring the sour taste of his breath. "You keep me grounded, you know that. I didn't mean to call you a dope. You are anything but."

Last year, before she'd kidnapped the whore nurse, Phillip had begged her to run away with him to start a new life in California. But she hadn't been able to abandon her daughter. Then things had gone terribly wrong. She should've listened to him.

She pressed her hips against his erection, another area where Blake ranked far superior to him. "You've done so much for me already. You're like my shining star. Do you still have that burner phone? I need to make some calls. Not right now though." She gyrated her hips and he rolled his hand over her ass. Dammit, he was ready for sex. At least she hadn't showered yet this morning. "Let's discuss this later. There's something more urgent on my mind right now."

~

THE RETURN ADDRESS on the shipping label read China. Blake could have failed to mention he was expecting a delivery. Likely he ordered something online, not realizing it was from out of the country. He wasn't fond of foreign-made products. But her name was listed in the recipient block, not his.

After the dead rose incident, he wouldn't try to surprise her with an anonymous package. Sure, she'd admired the red heels in the store window on the Boulevard last week when the three of them went for ice cream. And she'd lamented that her laptop was running slow of late and, when he asked, couldn't remember how old the thing was. But he'd buy those with her consent.

Written above her name and address were the words "A surprise for you." No, Blake wasn't behind this. Her hands fisted at her mouth, she stared at the box from across the room, and jumped when the doorbell rang. Kelly recognized the panic in her eyes.

"What is it?"

"An anonymous delivery. I don't think I should open it."

"Where?"

She led the way to the kitchen. "What the hell? Blake is on duty, correct?"

She nodded and reached out when Kelly lifted the box and shook it. "Do you think you should be doing that?"

Kelly shrugged. "If it was a bomb, it would've gone off by now. Where's a pair of scissors? I'm cutting this baby open. Otherwise both of us will wonder all day what the hell is in it."

Noreen stepped up beside her. "Maybe I should do it. I don't want you to get hurt."

"Girl, we're ready for it. Here, I'll hold it and you cut it open."

The rip of tape echoed through the silent house. Noreen lifted the right panel open first and then the left, peering beneath each flap. But the contents were covered by brown wrapping paper. Kelly moved her head closer as Noreen cautiously lifted the top layer.

"Oh my God," Kelly screamed.

Inside, a live tarantula crawled around in a nest of white gauze. Noreen stifled her scream, slapped the flaps closed, turned the box over on the table and reached for the cast iron skillet on the stove to weight it down. Fortunately, Blake had forgotten to put it away last night.

She backed away and began to tremble. "Jesus, Kelly. Why would someone send this?" She folded her hands and pressed them against her mouth, smashing beads of sweat on her upper lip. She stared at the box. Did it move? She held her breath and didn't blink until her eyes started to water. No. It stayed still.

Kelly's eyes popped but she regained her composure. "This is some crazy shit." Pressing on the skillet to hold it in place, she examined the package.

"It's just like the dead flowers. Not a clue about anything."

"I know."

"When did this arrive?"

She checked her watch. "About ten minutes before you. I had a bad feeling minutes after the doorbell rang and it wasn't you. I opened the door and the box was on the porch. This time I looked for a delivery person or van. But nothing and no one was around." The hairs on the back of her neck pinched. "I was going to leave it outside but changed my mind in case whoever delivered it was watching. Maybe I should've left it on the porch."

"No matter. I would have carried it in with me." Kelly propped her hands on her hips. "That's probably why there is tape over the doorbell."

Noreen gasped. "There is?"

"Yeah. I figured it must be out of order, but I pushed it anyway and it rang. Damn, someone thought this through enough to tape over the camera eye. I wonder if they thought about that when they walked up the steps. The surveillance tape might still show something."

She shook her head. "Lord, this is bold. Leaving it right at your door. I'll call the police. They can take this thing away before Gia sees it. You should call Blake."

"I hate to bother him at work."

"Girlfriend, something like this isn't bothering the man. He needs to know. Remember, you promised you'd let him know immediately if anything suspicious happened. What about this isn't suspicious?"

Despite her racing heart, she laughed. Before she could dial it, her phone rang from the kitchen counter. Another unknown caller. Her temper flared.

"What do you want? What the hell do you want from me?" There was only white noise on the other end. She stabbed the speaker button so Kelly could listen. Someone was there, breathing. She wouldn't be bested. "You don't scare me you son of a bitch." She disconnected the call.

"I'm dialing the police. You call Blake."

Her phone rang and simultaneously vibrated in her hand and she squealed. Jesus, she was jittery today. As if knowing something was amiss, Blake was calling. Her heart stuttered.

"Hey you, hi. I wanted to hear your voice before you left."

She smiled. Could he be more thoughtful? "Hi. It's nice to hear yours too."

"What's the matter?" No fooling this man. He detected the quiver in her words.

"Kelly and I just opened a box with a tarantula inside." His bellow likely caused the entire squad to jump to attention and rush to their lieutenant's office.

He had a hundred questions, none of which she wanted to answer. "No, I didn't see who delivered it. Yes, the security cameras are operating. No, they laid tape over it, but Kelly thinks we might see the person coming up the steps. No, up until the box arrived, it was a normal morning. I walked Gia into class and came straight home. Please, Blake, I just opened the thing. I'm still a little frazzled. Yes, Kelly is here. She's calling the police."

Blake released an audible sigh. "I understand. Sorry to press you like that." The tone of his voice hinted that he didn't understand. "I'll review the feed from the security cameras as soon as I hang up. Maybe we have a good shot of the bastard's face. Tell the police if an identity is viable, I'll make them a copy of the video. I know you two planned to go out, I can't remember where. Do you think that's advisable?"

"We don't want to miss the birthday party. As it is, we're going to be late if we have to wait for the police. I'm sure we'll be fine. We don't plan to stay long but Kelly was the little girl's assigned nurse and she wants to pop in and see her. I do too, for that matter." Their former patient wasn't expected to survive when she first rolled onto their floor and today, she turned five. The family invited the entire surgical recovery unit to the celebration."

"Okay. Please be careful. Call me after the police leave and tell me what they say. Take pictures from all angles before they take the evidence. Text me when you're leaving and when you get to the party. And reverse that on your way home."

His instructions of late were always to text him. It had taken her a while to realize that she spent very little time by herself since the car accident. Blake had activated an army of people who managed to have a reason to spend time with Noreen when she wasn't at the hospital and he wasn't home with her. She didn't think it was necessary, but she didn't refuse the company.

"I know the drill, don't worry. Would it be easier if I simply left the line open and you spent your entire day listening to mine?" She meant it jokingly. Almost.

Blake laughed. "I think I'd enjoy that. Sorry to be a nag. But one more thing."

"What?" It sounded harsher than she meant it to.

"Remember I love you."

The man had a way of calming her nerves and turning her bones to butter.

~

THREE HOURS LATER, the women buckled themselves into Kelly's car, grinning like happy clowns. She turned to Kelly.

"That was one of the most rewarding days of my career. My cheeks actually hurt from grinning so much."

"Girl, you don't have to tell me. Right now I feel like I could save the world."

She agreed. "What a nice party. She looks wonderful, don't you think? And her parents." She laid her hand over her heart. "My goodness, they practically gushed over us. It was almost embarrassing."

"I'll cherish every hug. Did you see that photographer walking around? I bet he snapped some great pictures."

"Yes, he kind of surprised me. A professional photographer for a five-year-old's birthday? But I guess when you come so close to losing your child a year earlier, you want it recorded for posterity."

"Well if you ask me, they could've recorded it a lot cheaper on their phones." Kelly waved her cell phone. "These babies take great pictures. Did you think there was anything, I don't know, funny about him?"

"The photographer?" Noreen shrugged. "No, not really. Why?"

"I can't pinpoint it exactly." Kelly scrolled her finger along the cell's screen. "I asked him for a business card and he didn't have one. And I'm searching now for his company and finding nothing. It seemed to me he aimed the camera more at us, you more so than me, than he did the kids and the birthday girl."

Noreen's stomach turned a tiny flip. "What d'you mean?"

"Every time I spotted him, he was focused on you. Or me and you once we sat down. He'd catch my eye, wink, and then turn the camera away. It didn't feel right."

Noreen took a deep breath. She hadn't imagined it. "I caught him aiming at me a couple of times too. But Blake has us all on edge about situational awareness and being tuned into our surroundings and conscious of the people around us and I thought, maybe, I was overreacting."

Kelly smacked her hand against her thigh. "I knew I wasn't seeing things. But who was he? And why was he there if he wasn't hired by the parents to commemorate their daughter's birthday? They certainly don't have a beef with you or me. And they probably have no connection to Blake's ex-wife. I mean, I guess they could but isn't that a stretch? We treated that patient long before Blake barreled his way onto our floor and into our lives."

Noreen smiled at the recollection and Kelly's possessiveness. "I love that you love him too."

"Yeah, well, I love him enough to tell him about today." She held up her phone for Noreen to see. "I did a little picture-taking of my own. Maybe Blake can do something with this."

The birthday photographer's smiling face stared back at Noreen.

17

B lake disconnected his call with the police sergeant. Still no leads or witnesses to Noreen's accident. The driver Noreen struck reported seeing her car swerve out of control, but not being shoved by another vehicle. He'd just driven onto the highway. It was a frustrating dead end. But he was convinced it wasn't an accident.

He stared at the photo on his cell phone of the man who'd taken pictures at a birthday party Noreen and Kelly attended. Dark-framed glasses, brown hair, and a mustache to envy. The kid looked too young to be able to grow a mustache that full.

Both women said he pointed his lens at them too often for him to feel comfortable about the man. But who the fuck was he? Was he somehow connected to Lynne? How the hell would she know about a former patient Kelly and Noreen cared for long before he and Noreen met? The dots didn't connect.

Blake laid his phone down and pressed his fingers into his forehead, locking his eyelids closed. What he wouldn't give for a scotch right now.

The women said it felt "creepy," but said it didn't seem suspicious. Maybe he was overreacting.

Kelly had contacted the parents and inquired about the photographer under the guise that the hospital might hire him for future events and after that phone call, she said he seemed on the up and up. A struggling photographer who was a friend of a friend of the birthday girl's father. The parents were extremely pleased with his work and encouraged Kelly to hire him. Another dead-end, like the accident.

Blake wasn't sure what he suspected. Of late, he was dubious of even a miss-delivered piece of mail. Noreen was right. His mind was working overtime. But two events involving a photographer taking pictures of Noreen, once in the park and at a birthday party, was questionable. Maybe it wasn't the man he needed to focus on.

He called for Joe.

"What's up, Lewey?"

"Can you show me the picture of the park photographer?"

In seconds, Joe's phone lay beside his.

"These men look different but the same. They appear to have the same facial structure, don't you think?"

"Kinda hard to tell from the side view I have. The man with Lynne at the park didn't wear glasses. Or have a mustache."

Blake's heart stuttered. "Forget the face. Look at the camera. Same exact camera used by both men. What are the odds?"

Joe's eyes narrowed. "I don't know much about photography. Maybe it's the top-of-the-line model that all professionals use. I can do some checking if you want."

"I doubt Lynne can afford a top-of-the-line anything." He spread the image on his phone with his two fingers. "That's really a healthy mustache. He barely looks like he needs to shave. The jawlines are identical. It could be a disguise."

Joe's eyes narrowed. "How are you making the leap from the photographer in the park to former ICU patients? Where does Lynne fit in?"

His head pounded behind his left eye. He sighed. "I don't

know. It's so thin it's anorexic. I'm going in circles. Yeah, if you have some time, see what you can find out about cameras."

Joe gave him a thumbs-up and left the office.

If he let his mind run, every recent event seemed suspicious. Next, he'd be questioning the rain.

He turned toward the baby doll perched on the filing cabinet at the back wall of his office. Add her to the "suspicious" column. He'd had a long talk with the principal at Gia's school, irate that a stranger had succeeded in approaching any child that closely and possibly gain access. The teacher's aide on duty that day was reprimanded and transferred. Noreen and Gia believed he'd disposed of the doll, but he stowed her in his office, hesitant to throw away anything that might be a key to...what? He wasn't sure.

At least he was certain the doll came from Lynne. But nothing else was adding up. Not the deliveries. Not the accident. Nothing. Lynne was living on her own now and the court expected him to cooperate with the supervised visits. The judge presiding over the case requested a sit-down with Gia but was involved in a lengthy custody trial. In the interim, and for continuity purposes according to the certified letter he received, another parental meeting was advised. It had worked well with Noreen attending as legal guardian, but this next visit was scheduled when she was at the hospital. She was going in early to cover for a co-worker. It was as if Lynne had Noreen's schedule and knew she was unavailable. How could that be?

Noreen offered to change her shift but instead, he'd rescheduled Joe, with Joe's enthusiastic permission. He and Brittni would take Gia to lunch with her mother this Saturday. Blake saw it as a show of force.

He hadn't told Gia about the appointment yet. Better to leave that to the last minute rather than watch his little girl sink into a black hole of dread.

His gaze returned to the doll. Her face was disturbing. Baby dolls were supposed to be cute, not sinister looking. He yanked the thing from the filing cabinet and walked to the window for brighter light. It was her eyes. Something was off with the doll's eyes. He shook it and one eyelid opened and closed. The other eye kept staring at him.

Blake reached for the letter opener and edged it into the corner, seeing the piece wiggle when touched. One pop and the part came out of the socket. What the fuck? Behind the plastic eyeball was a tiny lens, no bigger than a watch battery. He squinted at it in his palm. There were no wires in the socket and nothing protruding from the lens. A wireless transmitter? It couldn't be very powerful. Where was the receiver? Typical Wi-Fi coverage is about one-hundred feet in all directions.

Lynne had gone out of her way to put this doll in Gia's possession. Did she think she could monitor Gia's where-abouts? From where? She'd have to be closer than half of a football field with no obstructions or interference between her and the transmitter. A rainy day like today could cause issues. The signal likely wouldn't carry through the walls of Gia's school building and certainly if she were at home, Lynne would never get near enough to activate it.

How would Lynne know about a transmitter like this? She wasn't computer savvy, or technologically smart. If the thing did work, where and what was it transmitting back to? He lowered one slat of the window blind and peered out into the parking lot. The fire station property was surrounded by trees. It didn't lend itself to any type of surveillance.

Removing a magnifying glass from the desk drawer, he inspected the piece. If he could track the serial number, maybe he could determine the origin of purchase. And the buyer. That was a long shot at best. Man, he could use a drink.

He dropped the eyeball and lens in his pocket and plunked the doll back on its filing cabinet perch. Maybe the IT folks at City Hall would have some ideas.

EVEN THOUGH SCOOPS was her favorite place to go for ice cream, no amount of cajoling Saturday morning could convince Gia that lunch with her mother would be fun. Hell, the adults didn't believe it, so how could they convince a six-year-old? He spoke slowly, trying to explain the situation to his daughter, her face pressed into his neck. Sometimes, grown ups had to do things that were unpleasant, too. Gia didn't want the judge to get mad at him, did she? She had to be a big girl and help Daddy.

Gia demanded assurances that neither Joe nor Brittni would let go of her hand or leave her side. They promised not to force her to speak to her mother and that she could order anything she wanted from the menu for lunch, even a double order of chocolate ice cream. The bellyache would be worth it if it convinced Gia to go.

The look on his daughter's face when she climbed out of Joe's truck across from the ice cream shop crushed him. Her lower lip protruded, and her forehead stayed wrinkled. She clung to Brittni's hand, and pressed Mr. Fox and Mr. Dog to her chest. Joey laid his hand on the back of her head reassuringly.

He waited a block away from the ice cream parlor, sweating despite the air hiked up to the maximum level. He stared at the front door of the shop, afraid to blink, afraid he'd miss something. "Gentlemen start your engines," he whispered to no one when he saw Lynne approach the eatery.

He checked the time. As usual, Lynne was ten minutes late. If Gia was so important to her, why hadn't she been early? Or at least on time. Once she disappeared inside the ice cream shop, the minutes ticked by slower than Heinz ketchup rolling from its bottle. His imagination ran wild, visualizing Joe losing his temper and attacking Lynne, Brittni engaging in a catfight with her and worst of all, Lynne snatching Gia away from them and running from the restaurant. He was ready if that happened.

Less than five minutes into the meeting, the door flew open with a loud bang and Lynne ran out, waving her arms and screeching. From this distance, he couldn't hear what she said but based on body language, she was angry and hurling insults or worse. She pointed inside, pointed in the air, stomped her foot, and waved her phone. In front of her, a man wearing the company ice cream shirt stood blocking the doorway, his arms crossed over his chest, his stance defiant. Lynne shook her fist in his face.

Blake resisted the urge to rush there. Gia was safe with Joe and Brittni and he wasn't allowed near this visitation.

A patrol car rolled up, double-parked, and the flashing lights flicked on. The first time he and Gia met Noreen for ice cream here, Lynne summoned the police claiming he'd threatened her life. That was the day Noreen provided an alibi of sorts for him, the day he realized she was something special. Maybe Joe really had attacked her. He'd been mad enough.

He texted. *What's going on?*

All good. We're having lunch. Joey was the master of the understatement.

Lynne turned her rantings on the police officer. Her argument apparently failed because he escorted her across the street to the parking lot. Blake lost sight of her after that. The restaurant manager stood sentry at the door until the cop returned, slipped into the cruiser, turned off the lights and drove away.

Blake waited, wondering what means of transportation Lynne used to get there and whether or not her friend from the park was with her. It would've been nice to catch a license plate number. Maybe she was sitting in that lot, waiting for him to show his face. The tactic didn't seem beneath her. He stayed put.

About a half-hour later, the three of them emerged from the ice cream shop, Gia skipping between Joe and Brittni. His little darling looked as bright as the sunshine.

He waited beside the rear door and when she saw him, she flew into his arms.

"Daddy, lunch was fun. Mother was bad and the man who owns the restaurant made her leave. And I ate a whole plate of French fries all by myself."

Gia had a way of reminding him what was important in life.

He smiled, ignoring the sense of foreboding. "A whole plate? Did you eat anything else?"

Her curls bobbed when she shook her head and giggled. He tightened the seatbelt on her car seat. "Well, that means you eat something healthy for dinner, like a vegetable, okay?

"Okay. Will Weenie be home?"

"No, she's working. We're having dinner with Uncle Joey and Miss Brittni tonight. Does that sound fun?"

He wanted details about the day but held off until they were back at Joe's house and Brittni entertained Gia in the other room.

"She saw me first, but I'm not sure she recognized me right away. Gia was coloring on the placemat. The minute I stood up, Lynne started to scream. It scared the hell out of everybody in there, including me. She went crazy, screaming for me to get away from her daughter. I knew she was a lunatic but Brittni has never seen it. Her jaw dropped open, but she wrapped her arms around Gia and I don't think a pry bar could have loosened her grip." He grinned proudly.

Blake's heart warmed. These two were as close as family to him and Gia.

"The manager rushed over and all I said was we were there to chaperone a meeting with her daughter. By then, Lynne was out of control and he was having none of it. One table had already emptied. He told her to leave. He wasn't too gentle about it either. He grabbed her elbow and pushed her toward the door. Of course, she began screaming she'd sue him for assault. But he didn't back down and practically shoved her out the door. It was awesome."

"What was Gia doing through all this?"

"Brittni was whispering to her the whole time. She asked if you were coming and we reminded her that you were outside. Then we bribed her with the French fries. Sorry about that, Lewey, but it took her mind off what was going on."

He barely heard the apology. For every action, there is an equal and opposite reaction. What would Lynne do now?

"Lewey? You okay?"

"Were you able to find anything out about that camera?"

"No, nothing substantive. Not yet."

"Let me tell you what I found in that damn doll."

18

Lynne slammed the refrigerator door and handed Phillip the orange juice. "Can't you change your schedule? For God's sake, how many people actually want to work nights? I'd think your co-workers would jump at the chance to switch with you."

Watching him swig the drink from the bottle, she cringed.

"You have to be patient, babe. I haven't asked yet. I'm still in training."

How much training did a janitor require?

"And there's no guarantee I'll be assigned to her floor. I told you I didn't think this was a good plan."

"At least you're in the same building as her. That's a start."

"Yeah, well, I saw a lot of cameras around. Spying on her isn't as easy as you think."

"Don't be ridiculous. I strolled right into the ICU unit when she was in the hospital and no one gave me a second glance. Walked right up to her bed. I thought she was asleep or I'd have pounced faster. Seeing Argia curled up against her distracted me and that one-minute delay gave her the advantage."

Phillip wasn't in a sympathetic mood today. He slammed

the bottle on the counter. "Well then, what d'you need me for? You go back into that hospital and watch her if you're so good at this." He stormed from the room.

She was pushing him, maybe too hard. But he didn't understand the gravity of the situation. That woman was taking her place in her daughter's and her husband's life. She had to be eliminated.

That wasn't the only thing crawling under her skin. One of the provisions of her release was that she be gainfully employed. But she'd only ever worked part-time in that rental office where she met Blake. She'd quit not long after that so her experience was minimal.

She didn't anticipate earning more than minimum wage, which hardly paid for her tastes.

Phillip claimed he picked up odd handyman jobs, but she wasn't sure she believed that. It could account for his dirty fingernails. No matter. He had no regular flow of income. She wondered how he paid his rent before they took over this place, and was mortified to learn some months, he didn't. If a landlord evicted him, he mooched off his friends for a place to stay.

He was content to wander around most of the time snapping pictures of abstract things that caught his fancy, like the spokes on the rim of a high-end car, instead of working to establish himself as an artist. He certainly had the talent. But much to her dismay, his no-strings attitude spilled into no responsibility and no money in the bank.

He hadn't liked her suggestion that he apply for a job at the hospital. It had taken her many long talks and a lot of sex to coax him to do it.

At first, she considered the fire station. But he'd have to attend the academy and that would take too long. She doubted he'd pass the physical demands of the training, let alone the academic requirements. Or the drug test.

Then, she'd come up with the idea of him working at the

hospital as a janitor. No education or training needed. Easy to smuggle in the cup she peed in. And then, find Noreen Jensen. She already knew what floor the pediatric intensive care unit was on. Simply keep an eye on the whore-nurse and look for an opportunity to discredit her. She hadn't plotted the whole thing out but that didn't matter. She needed access to the woman and Phillip working in the hospital allowed that. Why didn't he understand that?

She walked out to the deck and handed him a cold beer. "I'm sorry. I have to find a job and you are so employable, I guess I'm a little jealous." She repressed a gag. "I know you only took this janitorial job to make me happy. I know you'd do anything for me, and I can't love you enough to show my appreciation." She ran her hand down his back to his sagging jeans. "I'm on edge and I'm taking it out on you. They say you only hurt the ones you love."

Phillip's face remained rigid. He took the beer without looking at her and chugged half of it. She stepped close enough for her breasts to rub his arm, but his eyes were hard when he finally turned.

"I've got to get ready for work."

PHILLIP PRESSED his fists into his eyes to stop the negative thoughts. He was tired of her. Always pushing, obsessed by the nurse and the little brat. It wasn't the woman who needed to disappear. If she was ever going to act sane again, the kid had to go.

What was it about Lynne that he couldn't walk away from? She was fun at first, the most adventurous older woman he'd ever known. Not so hot when she scrubbed her face at night but after time in front of her makeup mirror, she was a knockout. He was proud to go out with her. His friends dubbed her the Crazed Cougar after her arrest last year. Yeah, she liked to put on airs, like she was better than everyone else. She wasn't.

But he let her carry on as if she were. Hell, he'd been laid more times since meeting her than his entire life. She liked sex in public places and he'd admit, the danger of getting caught in a parking lot or the bathrooms at the park was a rush for him too. He wouldn't mind a repeat in the men's room at his favorite Mexican restaurant.

Her body was showing signs of age, her breasts starting to sag and her ass jiggling when she didn't squeeze into the shapers or whatever she called them. He'd never tell her that, though. She strutted around as proud as an eighteen-year-old.

More than a year ago, he'd come on to her in the auto parts store thinking she had money. She dressed like it, acted like it and he wasn't above being kept by a woman. The first time he saw her house he was floored. Two stories and full of quality furnishings, including a grand piano in pristine condition. Praise Jesus, he thought he'd tapped a gold mine.

She was fighting some crazy divorce, trying to win back her daughter. He didn't care then. She literally opened her legs and her wallet for him in exchange for a couple favors—track her ex's truck, bolt the basement door, abandon a car behind a shopping center. It didn't matter what she asked, he was happy to oblige. She promised there was a pot of gold at the end of the yellow brick road. Or something like that.

Then she went crazy and set the house on fire. With the nurse and kid inside. She claimed to this day it was an accident, but he knew better. Her ex and that nurse pushed her over the edge. He was just grateful he wasn't around that day to get caught up in her mess.

Yet, watching that house burn, seeing them drag that woman out on a stretcher, everyone holding their breath because it looked like she'd checked out—it was a rush. Unlike any speed or crack he'd ever tried.

Yeah, Lynne was crazy, but she was a helluva ride. She fascinated him, which had to explain why he hung around after her arrest. Detainment, she preferred to call it. She was like watching a high wire act perform without a net. He waited, mesmerized, to see her crash and burn.

If she would've listened to him, they could be on the West Coast right now with her ex pumping alimony checks into her bank account monthly. But her ego bested her better judgment.

Today, she was poorer than him and working her way out of the criminal justice system. That's one thing he could brag about, he'd didn't have a record. Never been caught although he'd come close. But his nose was clean.

Lynne was jeopardizing that, though, concocting outrageous revenge schemes, dragging him down that road with her. It was getting old. He'd been happy to go along with scaring the nurse, calling her from burner phones, and taking a road-rage trip down the highway to intimidate her. He'd only tapped her back bumper a couple times. He hadn't expected her to veer off the road like that. Secretly, he was glad she survived.

At the park, he'd watched her with the kid, and she seemed nice. The kid was having a ball playing until Lynne showed up. Why did she want that brat around anyway? Just to prove a point? It wasn't his point to prove and he was bored with being Lynne's puppet.

He snapped his timecard in the hospital employee clock and ambled through the double doors. Now she had him working as a janitor, trying to make his way to the pediatric floor where the nurse worked. Eight hours of cleaning up other people's mess. Cleaning up Lynne's mess.

It wasn't a rush anymore.

19

Noreen nodded to the maintenance man mopping the floor at the employee's entrance. He wore a ball cap drawn low over his forehead and he kept his focus on the tiles in front of his feet. Odd that he wore a hat. That wasn't part of the uniform for that department, but her brain was too weary first thing Monday morning to concern herself about it. She jabbed the elevator button for the pediatrics floor.

She'd switched shifts to work a half-day today. Gia's meeting with the judge was this afternoon, the one-on-one session he'd insisted upon. It had been a tense weekend. "Don't coach her," their attorney had warned. "If the judge asks if her daddy told her to say something and she says yes, it's a strike against you. It implies you attempted to influence her."

They'd waited until yesterday to tell her about the appointment, but Blake had been on edge since coming home Saturday morning and Gia sensed it. She was so tuned into her father, he could have a hangnail and she'd complain her finger hurt.

It didn't help that he'd dropped a glass in the living room Saturday night and it shattered. He said it was an accident, but she'd watched him throw back scotch after scotch and suspected he'd been on the verge of passing out when the tumbler slipped from his hand. She'd been trying unsuccessfully to keep Gia distracted but even her favorite princess movie didn't hold her attention and when the glass crashed to the floor, Gia burst into tears and Blake scolded her. That moment brought tears to everyone's eyes.

Noreen leaned against the back wall as the elevator doors closed and filled her lungs with air, held it a few seconds, and released it slowly through her mouth. Sunday hadn't gone any better. All three of them were cranky and picked at each other.

She exhaled another deep breath. She felt guilty leaving the house this morning for the short shift, but this unit was a tight-knit group that watched each other's backs. Her co-worker needed the morning for personal matters and didn't have the vacation time to take off. Noreen offered to work the first half of her shift. At least this took her temporarily out of the house, and these would be six welcomed hours when someone else's challenges could occupy her brain.

One hour later, the maintenance man with the hat stepped off the elevator. No mop or bucket this time. He looked up and down the hallway before nodding to her at the desk. "Wrong floor. Sorry."

She rose from her chair and squinted as the elevator doors slowly closed. Her heartbeat zoomed. He looked just like the photographer who'd been with Lynne at the park. And his voice was familiar. He sounded like the man who'd been snapping pictures at the birthday party.

FOR THE PAST FEW WEEKS, the new car smell made her smile every time she stepped into the shiny white compact SUV. Today, she drove home in a dark mood, questioning her recollection. The odds of the photographer being the same as the employee she saw were beyond slim. It certainly wasn't the best day to discuss it with Blake. He hadn't slept last night. He wasn't likely to be in a good mood this afternoon.

She'd wait until they were outside the judge's chambers, waiting for Gia's meeting to end. She'd tell him then about the similarities between the two men. Maybe the distraction would be good for him.

She released the breath she didn't know she held when laughter drifted her way after she opened the door from the garage to the kitchen. Blake sat at the table with a spoon dangling from his nose while Gia erupted in giggles.

Gia jumped up and ran to her. "Weenie, look at daddy!" The spoon crashed to the table when Blake smiled and rose to walk toward her. This was her family. A six-year-old who clung to her thighs and a man who looked at her like no one ever had. All darkness disappeared. She embraced them with her arms and her heart.

Blake dropped a sweet kiss on her lips. "Hi. Welcome home."

Gia spun in a circle in front of her. "Weenie, look at my new dress. It's for the judge to see how grown up I am."

She sensed her eyebrows raise. "You look mighty grown up. I don't recognize that but it's really pretty."

Gia clapped her hands. "Me and Daddy bought it."

An impish smile graced Blake's face and he shrugged. "Shopping always makes a woman feel better, doesn't it?"

Noreen's heart fluttered. "Coming home to you does the trick too. I'll change and we'll go."

IN THE TRUCK on the way to the courthouse, Gia conversed non-stop with Mr. Fox and Mr. Dog, telling them they'd have to wait in the truck but if they were good, her dad had promised ice cream treats tonight.

Noreen smiled. "Shopping and ice cream. Anything else I should know?"

Blake lips edged upward. "Only that we love you, don't we Gia?" Over Noreen's shoulder, chestnut curls bobbed. The closer they drove to their destination, the tighter her stomach cinched. She silently prayed. *Dear Lord, please let this go our way.*

The trio walked hand in hand from the parking lot. Blake cleared his throat. "Remember to be polite, Gia. And do your best to answer the judge's questions."

Gia's arms swung back and forth. "Don't worry, Daddy. Uncle Joey helped me know what to say."

Blake halted. "What d'you mean Uncle Joey helped you?"

Gia giggled and tugged on his hand. "Uncle Joey said the judge wants to know who I love. That's easy, Daddy. I love you and Weenie and Mr. Fox and Mr. Dog and Grammy and Uncle Joey and Miss Brittni and my teachers and Miss Jenny's puppy and Santa Claus 'cause he brings me presents and the Easter Bunny because he brings me candy and the Tooth Fairy 'cause she leaves me a surprise under my pillow and Princess Ariel and Belle and," she paused to catch her breath, "and Weenie what's the one I can't member, the one who is Anna's sister?"

Noreen swallowed hard seeing Blake's eyes rimmed with tears. "Elsa, honey. Her name is Elsa."

Gia's head bobbed. "Don't worry, Daddy. I'll tell the judge who I love."

20

T wo days later, Noreen studied the elevator doors every time the bell pinged and they opened. Kelly noticed.

"What's up, girlfriend? Are you waiting on our man?" She did an impromptu dance in a circle with her arms in the air chanting "Blake, Blake, he's our man."

"I'm waiting on *a* man, not ours. I'm not one-hundred percent certain why, though."

Kelly's brow wrinkled.

Noreen inhaled heavily. She hadn't had the chance to tell Blake about the resemblance the maintenance man bore to Lynne's friend. He'd run into another fireman in the hallway right after the judge's assistant escorted Gia into chambers. They'd chatted for what seemed like forever and then she'd gotten a phone call from the hospital. By then, Blake was pacing non-stop, consumed with his own fears. He scooped up Gia the minute she emerged from the office and the rest of the night had been devoted to his princess.

She'd proudly announced that she couldn't tell either of them what she and the judge discussed, declaring it was a secret between them. She did say he was "a very nice man." Noreen hadn't wanted to spoil the mood of the night with concerns about the janitor. She was probably overreacting anyway.

Kelly's eyes pierced holes into her. "Talk to me."

"There was a maintenance worker on our floor the other day, the morning I worked the half day." She dropped her head into her hands and squeezed her temple between her thumbs. "I don't know, Kelly, it sounds crazy to say it out loud."

"Crazy is my middle name, child. Say it."

She raised her gaze to her friend's face. "I saw him mopping downstairs. And then later, he stepped off the elevator on our floor. He said it was the wrong floor and got right back on. But he stood out, that is I noticed him because he wore a ball cap. He had it on when I saw him mopping."

"A ball cap?" Kelly's voice climbed an octave. "Ain't no employees in this building who wear ball caps."

"I know. It struck me as peculiar. The hat caught my attention so I only caught a glimpse of his face, but..."

"But what?"

"He looked like the photographer who was at the birthday party. It was the hat that caught my eye. In the pictures from the park, he wore his hat low over his eyes. The bill was severely curved. At the birthday party, he had it turned backward. But the bill was curved. The guy who was mopping the floors had the same curved bill." She arced her hands in front of her forehead imitating the shape. "It's the same guy."

Before Kelly could interrupt, she added, "At least I think it is. I'm not certain. It's crazy to think he'd be working here but there was something about him...I can't explain it. That's why I'm watching the elevator. I'm hoping to see him today for a better look."

Kelly rolled her eyes. "That's like waiting for it to rain when the sun is shining. Did you see a name or anything on his uniform?"

Noreen shook her head.

"And you say he was doing the floors? Not wiping windows or pushing the bathroom carts? How the hell did he get up here? This is a secure floor."

"I don't know how he got up here. When I saw him downstairs near the time clock, he was mopping. He didn't have a bucket or mops with him when he got off the elevator here. Not that I saw, anyway."

Kelly drummed her fingers on the countertop. "That doesn't sound right. Granted, this is an easy building to get lost in but no one comes to this floor unauthorized. Not even the cleaning people. Where was his bucket? Seems odd. When I take my lunch break, I'll run down to maternity. My friend Christine works that floor and she's friendly with someone in the personnel office. She never really said they're dating but I kinda think that's the deal. HR can't know.

"No matter. Maybe I can do some digging and find out who this guy is. Maintenance has assignments just like we do. Did you tell Blake about him?"

"No, I couldn't. The timing wasn't right. I saw the man the same morning of Gia's meeting with the judge. Blake was a jumble of nerves until it was over and then, he was like a different man. Like he didn't have a care in the world. And I knew I wasn't working again until today so there was no imminent danger. I wasn't going to spoil his good mood for any of us."

Kelly agreed.

"See if Christine's friend can help us. It might be a wild goose chase. I'll tell Blake as soon as I get home tomorrow."

21

Phillip sucked on the joint, filled his lungs to capacity, closed his eyes and reclined the driver's seat. Lynne was out of control. Screaming like a mad woman in the apartment, throwing dishes, ash trays, whatever she laid her hands on. Thank God his cameras were locked in the trunk, along with his laptop, his stash of cash and some of his clothes. Come to think of it, he moved more and more of his stuff out of the apartment each day.

He exhaled loudly and took another hit. Dammit, he should've checked the mail before handing it to Lynne. She tore open the letter from the court and screeched like a banshee as she read it. Christ, he might have permanent ear damage.

Spit flew from her mouth when she yelled, "I'll kill her." At first, he thought she meant the kid, which made no sense. She said she did everything she did for the kid. Then she asked if he had a gun. Or could get a gun. What the fuck? Was she outta her mind?

So what if the court ruled against her? He didn't want the little brat running around the place anyway. Life was much easier with just the two of them, sleeping late, eating take-out at midnight, and screwing anywhere anytime. Why couldn't Lynne see that would all change if they had to babysit? Why didn't she believe that if the kid came to stay, he'd leave? She laughed when he said that the other night, before the Letter from Hell arrived.

"Where would you go?" She threw her head back and opened her mouth so wide, he saw to the back of her throat. Gross. He flinched like he was seeing it again and took another hit of the joint.

What'd she know anyway? As if he didn't have any place to crash. Hell, there were ten doors he could knock on right now. Ten places he could crash, no strings attached.

So why didn't he? The sex? Yeah, that was part of it. Living on the edge of insanity—more like with insanity—was a rush. A front row seat to madness on a stage that he stepped on and off at will, sometimes as an actor and other times as an audience member. But every show eventually ends.

He helped her last time not realizing she would try to kill that nurse. Yeah, Lynne could deny till she was blue in the face settin' that fire with the nurse and the kid down there, but he knew her well enough to know the truth. She snapped that day, for whatever reason. He hadn't been there, thank God.

He'd sweated the whole time she was in custody that she'd implicate him in her crazy scheme, which she never fully explained to him. Fuck, if he'd known the car she asked him to leave behind that shopping center wasn't really for a friend to pick up, he'd have told her to get screwed. He was little more than a petty criminal with no desire to become a felon.

He musta been really stoned that day. She could've burned him if she wanted. Was she crazy enough to keep records? Detailed shit she could use against him? It had been some tense weeks, waiting.

But she protected him, through the court proceedings and

everything. And for reasons he couldn't explain, he hung around. Like some battered woman, too afraid to leave.

Now, like quicksand pulling him under, he was sinking into another one of Lynne's sinister plots targeting the nurse. That's who she meant when she read the letter and screamed "I'll kill her."

Not the kid. No, the night after the meeting at the park, she'd ranted about how easy it would be to snatch the kid and leave the country. He didn't bother to point out that it wouldn't be so easy. She didn't have a passport that he was aware of. She was on probation and required to report in regularly plus attend some kind of therapy sessions. He never asked why she was going where he dropped her off. He didn't really care.

But her rage and insanity level were escalating now.

Kidnapping? Killing? She wasn't that good a lay.

He jerked the seat upright and turned the key in the ignition. Best to leave now, while she was distracted, and he was sure that's what he wanted to do. Out of the corner of his eye, he saw her. What the fuck was she doing? Braless in a shirt that could be her daughter's, thong panties and fuck-me stilettos. Swinging those hips as she walked toward the car. Jesus, did she want the other tenants to see her? Their apartment was on the second floor, for gawd's sake. Just like the first time he saw her, his erection jumped to attention. That was the real reason he endured all her crap.

Lynne leaned into the open driver's window and grinned. "I know you get horny when you smoke." Her tongue took a slow trip around her lips. "Come inside now."

Yeah, it might be time for this show to end. But the curtain didn't have to drop today.

～

NOREEN LAY on her back staring at the bedroom ceiling fan as it lazily looped in a counterclockwise circle. She flexed her toes beneath the sheet and fanned out her fingers. She was weightless. Not a care in the world since the court order arrived yesterday. Blake felt it. Even Gia sensed the change in their moods. Last night, she giggled at everything, lightening Noreen's heart even more. She declared the pasta spirals reminded her of her Slinky and tried to walk the slippery noodles on the table. She laughed and blew bubbles in her chocolate milk and laughed harder when Blake blew bubbles in his iced tea. She chose a princess movie she described as "the happiest."

Noreen drew in a deep breath and leaked it from her lungs. After meeting with Gia, the judge temporarily awarded full custody to Blake, pending the restoration of a relationship with the mother. He authorized supervised visits with Lynne once a week for one hour at a neutral location. She, Blake, or a guardian of his choice were authorized to accompany Gia and at any time that any one of them deemed the meeting was too stressful for Gia, they could end it. Likewise, the supervising caseworker had the authority to terminate any session she deemed unproductive or at which the worker felt Lynne was acting inappropriately.

Lynne was restricted from buying any presents or passing any items to Gia without Blake's approval. And there could be no contact with Gia between the scheduled visits.

Lynne had to be tearing out her hair.

The judge scheduled a follow-up session with Gia in six weeks, declaring that the progress made during that time between Lynne and Gia would highly weight his decision regarding permanent custody. It was interesting that the judge chose to communicate directly with a six-year-old instead of Blake or Lynne. Gia must have been something in that private meeting in chambers. What she wouldn't have given to be a fly on the wall.

This was a major victory, if only temporary. Until Lynne was completely out of their lives, she knew better than to fully relax. How many setbacks could Lynne take before...she didn't complete the thought. She was incapable of sinking to the depths Lynne had reached.

Pans clanked and Gia's soft laughter drifted from the kitchen. Sounded like she and Blake were making breakfast. There'd be a mess to clean up, but she and Blake would happily work side by side in the kitchen to complete the task. And she had the day to spend with them before reporting to work tonight. For now, their lives could return to normal.

HOURS LATER, she met Kelly in the parking lot as they reported to work. Kelly dispensed with the usual greetings, grabbed Noreen's forearm, and started talking. "He's a new hire. A temp. Doesn't have much of an employment history. Seems to jump around from job to job when he works. There are huge gaps in between gigs. But no criminal background. He's twenty-seven, not married and lives in an apartment on the east side. Adam and I took a drive yesterday afternoon and rode by the place. But everything was quiet. It's not in the best neighborhood. No where I'd let Gia go."

Noreen chuckled. Kelly and Adam were suited for each other. Their hearts embraced everyone. "Oh, Kelly. Now you're involving your boyfriend in my nightmare. Adam probably thinks I'm a kook."

Kelly rolled her eyes. "He's as worried about you as I am."

They scanned the halls while they punched their timecards and waited for the elevator but didn't see any unfamiliar faces. And no one mopping.

"Did you find out his name?"

"Yes. Phillip Santune. Do you recognize it?"

Noreen rolled the name around in her brain, robotically exiting the elevator and making her way to the horseshoe desk. She stashed her purse in the lower drawer and tugged her bottom lip in between her teeth. Inexplicably, she wanted to be familiar with the man, know him from school or the old neighborhood. Anything that wouldn't make him Lynne's friend. Something that would justify the feeling that she'd seen him before. The name didn't help.

"No. Off the top of my head, I'm drawing a blank."

Kelly removed two folded sheets from her purse. "Christine printed the information for me. There's one personal reference listed, but the file noted they couldn't reach the woman. Guess they hired him anyway." She studied the second sheet. "It's no wonder. This handwriting is barely legible." She drew the page closer to her face. "Looks like Fran Francis. Who the hell names their baby that?"

She shrugged and thrust the pages toward Noreen. "Maybe that's not what it says. See if you can make it out. I'll check the charts and see what our night looks like."

Noreen barely had time to glance at the employment application when a heart monitor signaled an alert. She turned the papers upside down on the desk and rushed to her patient.

Upon her return, Joe, Rob, and Kelly bent over the printouts. It was useless to protest sharing the information with these two. They were the closest to brothers Blake might ever have. She got right to the point.

"Either of you know him?"

The men shook their heads. "I just dialed the phone number but it went to voice mail." Joe grinned. "I left a message for my good buddy Phil to call me."

"What're you going to do if he does?"

His grin expanded. "I'll wing it."

Noreen's shoulders relaxed. It was hard to be afraid of anything surrounded by these people who would die for her.

Joe had gone without food and sleep when she and Gia were missing. He extended the first page toward her.

"Did you check his phone number with the calls you received?"

She hadn't thought of that but no sooner did she retrieve her phone from her purse and unlock it than a child began screaming. She threw the phone to Joe and ran down the hall behind Kelly, directing her words over her shoulder "You check."

By the time the emergency was resolved, the paramedics were gone. Noreen found a note on top of her phone in Joe's handwriting.

"The numbers match. We're following up. Please be extremely careful."

"Whaaattt?" Kelly's squeal echoed through the halls.

Noreen scrolled down the log of her recent phone calls. There were some deviations, but Joe was right, the number listed as Philip Santune's personal cell appeared at least ten times. She wasn't crazy.

22

J oe burst through the door before Blake could respond to his knock. "Lewey, we're on to something. I'm not sure what."

Typical Joey, he was breathless and speaking in sentence fragments. Blake raised his right hand outward. "Easy, Joe. Did you run here?"

Joe flattened his hands against Blake's desk and leaned forward on his elbows. "Yeah, I did. We found one of Noreen's anonymous callers. He's working at the hospital as a janitor. Not sure yet how he knows Lynne or what he is to her exactly, but Noreen says he looks like the dude who was with Lynne in the park that day."

Blake jumped up. "Whoa, Joey, slow down. Who are you talking about? Where's this guy now?' A cold chill rushed up his spine. Even through the confusion of Joe's words, a sense of dread began to squeeze his gut.

He listened while Joe spilled details about an employee Noreen was suspicious of, his heartbeat increasing as the impact of Joe's words hit home.

It was hard to believe Lynne could orchestrate something like this. But he believed Noreen.

"I'm gonna track this guy down, Lewey. We're off tomorrow morning. I'll have two days."

"Now wait a minute, Joe, you can't do that. For one thing, this isn't your problem. For another, if he is connected to Lynne, which begs a hundred questions like how does she know him? What is he to her? Is he a criminal too? Whoever he is, we don't want to spook him. And—"

Joe cut him off. "On the other hand, we can't take the chance that he is associated with your ex and gunning for Noreen. And you can't get involved because that puts you right where Lynne wants you, in front of the judge on a trumped-up harassment charge or worse." He pounded the desktop with his fist.

"And don't insult me by saying this isn't my problem. Don't discard the feelings I have, we all have for you and your family. They're our family too. Dammit, Lewey, hurt one of us, hurt us all. I'm gonna find this guy and figure out what he's up to. Don't forget, Brittni spends a lot of time with Gia so I have a right to be worried." He pointed a shaky index finger at Blake. "Your job is to take care of Noreen and Gia. I'll let you know what I find out."

He turned before Blake could say anything and slammed the office door behind him. Joe was absolutely right, and he was an ass. Check your ego, Matthews. You're part of a team. There is no I in that word.

Up until now, he didn't worry about Noreen when she was at work. He couldn't afford that luxury anymore. But what the hell was going on?

The fire alarm sounded, taking his attention off Noreen, and emergencies the rest of the night kept the entire crew busy. Blake apologized and said goodbye to Joe in the morning, not asking any more questions about his plans. It was better if he didn't know.

NOREEN WAS TIDYING up Gia's room when she heard Blake arrive. As always, butterflies danced in her stomach when he came home to her. He looked hot in his fireman's uniform. She might enjoy helping him take it off. She floated into his arms to deliver a warm kiss, her arms wrapping around his neck.

She eyed the box he carried. It was wrapped in plain brown paper. "Whatcha got?'

He filled his lungs with air. Was he nervous?

"Something for you. It's not a present though, so don't get excited. It's for your safety. Come in the kitchen with me."

She followed him, admiring the view from behind. The smile on her face disappeared when he removed the wrapping paper and opened the box to reveal a gun. She gasped.

"It's a Smith & Wesson. It's perfect for a woman's hand." He said it so matter-of-factly, she jerked her gaze up at him.

"Have you ever shot a gun before?"

She seemed to have lost her ability to speak. She stared alternately at him and the weapon.

"Guns are nothing to be afraid of if they are in the right hands. We'll keep it out of Gia's reach, but she already knows never to touch my weapons. I want you to carry it whenever you're without me. Even when you have Gia with you."

She whispered her words. "Blake, are you serious?"

"Very."

Her hand flew to her throat. "I've never even held a gun before. I can't shoot one."

"No, not right now you can't. You can take a day-long class. My friend runs an academy. Me teaching you is like a husband teaching a wife to drive. A sure fail plan."

She stared at the shiny pistol. "I-I don't think I can."

Blake ran his hand across her shoulders. "Yes, you can. You just have to get used to it. This is unloaded. Here, take it."

Her hand trembled when she reached for it. "Hold it with a firm grip." His hand wrapped around hers, pressing the gun into her palm. The handle felt rough. And heavy. He gently eased her forefinger off the grip and placed it alongside the barrel. "Always keep this finger here, straight. That way, you're ready to shoot." She'd never be ready.

"Support it with your other hand. Like a cup in a saucer." He raised her left hand and cupped it around her right. "How does it feel?"

Like she wanted to throw up. "It's heavy."

"Yeah, at first it is. You'll get comfortable with it."

"I-I don't know about this. I'm not sure it's a good idea."

Blake took the gun and laid it on the counter. He turned her shoulders toward him and raised her chin with his finger. "You're in danger. You need to be able to protect yourself. And Gia. I'm asking you to do this for both our sakes. We can't afford to lose you. We wouldn't be able to go on." He drew her into his embrace and kissed her forehead. "You'll take the training, and you won't even think about having it with you all the time. Let me show you some basics."

23

Phillip gagged at the lingering smell of disinfectant that clung to his fingers. Cleaning floors at the hospital sucked. The stink from it never went away. It was locked in his nose and he smelled it when he smoked. He needed a beer and time to think. This thing with Lynne had run its course. And whoever the hell was riding his bumper better back the fuck up.

For a third time, he checked his rearview mirror. Yeah, the black truck was definitely on his tail. Who knows? Maybe the crazy bitch was having him followed.

He coasted into his usual parking spot at the bar. A couple beers before his shift started at the Hellspital might get him through the night. Or get him fired, which would be okay too. Hell was the correct word for this hospital gig. Cleaning up other people's shit was not for him. He was above that.

The fucking black truck cruised into the parking lot and rolled to the last parking space. Whatever.

He strode into the rustic saloon, pausing for his eyes to adjust to the dark, and took his regular seat at the bar. The bartender acknowledged him with a nod and placed a draft in front of him, which was spotlighted in a beam of light when the door opened behind him. Just as he wrapped his fingers around the icy mug handle, a man sat right beside him. Was the dude blind? Every seat at the bar was empty. He didn't bother to look up.

"How ya doin' today?"

Maybe if he ignored the guy, he'd bother someone else.

"You work at the hospital, don't you?"

Phillip's heart ticked a beat quicker. He leveled his gaze on the foamy head of his beer and took a hefty swig. As the cool liquid slid down his throat, he turned to eyeball the intruder. Something vaguely familiar about the kid.

"What d'you care where I work?"

The guy frowned. "I don't. Not really. Thought I recognized you from there. That's all."

He narrowed his focus. "Do I know you?"

"Nah. I'm a friend of Lynne's."

A heart burst exploded in his chest like fireworks. He straightened. "That why you're following me? She hire you? She's nuts, you know. A certified whack job."

He stood and dug in his pocket for his cash. He didn't want anything to do with any friend of Lynne's. Dealing with her was enough.

The guy grabbed his arm to stop him. "Take it easy, man. I just want to talk to you. She didn't send me." He tugged, coaxing him to sit down again.

"Let me buy you another beer, man. I just want to shoot the shit with you."

"I gotta go to work."

The guy checked his watch. "Yeah? What time do you have to clock in because you're either late for the three o'clock shift or have time for one more before the four."

"Whaddaya want from me? I don't know you."

He signaled the bartender for another round. "No, no you don't. I only want to talk to you."

"What about?"

"About Lynne Matthews."

An ache started to throb in his brain. She was the last thing he wanted to talk about. "That woman is crazy. I'm getting' outta there this weekend. Just working through the end of the week so I can collect a full paycheck and then I'm quittin' that fuckin' hospital job too."

The guy nodded sympathetically. "I hear ya. It can't be fun. I hate hospitals." He gestured toward the fresh brew. "This will help. Make the job a little easier to take."

The second beer was colder and tasted better. Always did when someone else paid. Had he eaten anything today? He couldn't remember. He woke up and finished last night's joint. He'd needed it to put up with Lynne's ranting about the nurse. It was as if he hadn't closed his eyes from the night before, when she was on her rampage. She took up right where she left off the minute he lifted his lids. Ordering him to make something happen. Demanding he come home today with information she could use. What information? What the hell was he supposed to be looking for? He wasn't her lackey, dammit.

He drank half the mug on his second gulp and leaned back in his chair to study his benefactor. Who was he? What was his game? "Do I know you?"

Again, the guy shook his head. "Where is Lynne now?"

Why'd he want to know that? "You're her friend. Don't you know?"

"We lost touch when she went into the mental hospital. I heard she got out and was in rehab, but I can't find her."

That was good to hear. They'd both done a good job of laying low, except where the kid was concerned. Even before she went away, she didn't have any friends that he knew of. Certainly not any men friends. What was this guy's angle?

"Whaddaya want with her? How do you even know I know her?"

"I've been asking around about her. Someone said you might be able to help me."

"Yeah? Who?"

The guy sure didn't lose his cool. Just shrugged and said "someone."

"You lookin' to cause her trouble?"

The guy shot up straight and raised both hands, palms toward Phillip like he was a cop arresting him. "Nothing like that, man, no way. She asked me to hold onto some things for her before they sent her away. I figure she might need them now. That's why I'm trying to find her."

"What kind of things?"

The dude shrugged and tried to act dumb. "Just some things." He ordered two more beers.

"Give them to me. I'll see she gets them."

"I'd kind of like to see her, you know? See how she's doing. Besides, I don't know what you are to her. How do I know I can trust you?"

Now he was curious. Everything Lynne owned burned up in the house and she burned everything she brought from the rehabilitation house the first night she was out. "She's living with me, dude. She ain't got no one else but me."

His eyebrows came together to form a monobrow. "You just told me you were getting out of there. What d'you mean? You gonna dump her? Walk out on her if you're the only one she has? Is she that bad? I remember her as a real looker."

Phillip reached for the fresh beer. "Yeah, she still looks good when she makes the effort. She's great in the sack, too. But her obsession with gettin' her kid back has turned her ugly. I can't take it anymore."

What kind of things did this guy have that belonged to Lynne? Jewelry he could pawn? Money?

"What d'you have for her?"

The guy ignored his question. "Her kid? Someone told me she lost custody of that kid. How's she think she's going to get her back?"

"She's got some wild ass plans, let me tell you. But I'm done with it. I ain't never been arrested and I don't plan to be." A chill straightened Phillip's spine. "You ain't a cop are you?"

The guy answered quickly. "No, no, man. It'd be illegal to buy you beers and then question you. I'm just trying to find out what Lynne's up to, that's all. I got some cash for her. Not much but it'll help, especially if you're bailing on her. Doesn't matter to me if I give it to you or her, as long as I unload it. It might help."

"You mean help me?"

"Possibly."

"How much money are you talkin'?"

"Why? You want to stiff her? Are you that done with her?"

"I been supportin' her crazy ass for months. I'm entitled to re-payment. How much?"

The dude leaned in closer. "Let's talk about a deal."

24

Phillip left a note leaning against the glass fruit bowl. Lynne smashed it against the wall. "Who does he think he is? That little pissant."

The windows were open and the neighbors likely heard the breaking glass and her shriek, but she didn't care. The piece of shit left her. She hurled the glass vase with fake flowers at the door. "Walk out on me you little bastard? Like hell you will."

Anger blurred her vision when she looked around the no-frills apartment. This apartment was income assistance housing. His friend's furniture was dirty, with burn holes and stains. Even the roof over her head leaked. She didn't belong here.

She eyed the one-hundred-dollar bill on the floor. How had he come up with that? She went through his pockets most nights and rarely found anything larger than a twenty.

"For your expenses," his note had said. The little son of a bitch. What was she supposed to do after that?

Her efforts to find a job had been futile with her limited work experience. She wasn't familiar enough with computer programs and online networking to ease back into a desk job. Vocational training was part of her rehabilitation requirements, and she'd tried some classes at Dalton House. Fran had spent time with her at the computer, giving her basic instructions. That's how she'd searched for Argia's doll. But the technology of the Internet escaped her.

She'd gone on one job interview for a receptionist at a dentist's office thinking the tight skirt and plunging neckline was all she'd need. The questions they asked were ridiculous. What did it matter how many words she could type in a minute? Or if she was familiar with spreadsheets or search engines. She'd had to ask what a search engine was. The twenty-minute appointment was a dismal failure.

The other positions that Fran kept suggesting, like cashiering at the supermarket, were beneath her. Fran had said it was imperative that she find a job soon. She knew that. Yet she remained unemployed.

She relied on Phillip's drug deals to pay the bills. He thought she didn't know about that little business he operated out of his car. She could easily call the police on him this minute. Let his ass sit in jail. She wouldn't even visit him.

She'd do it. As soon as she calmed down. No sense sounding like an angry rejected woman when she phoned.

His note shook in her trembling hand. "I HAD ENOUGH. HERE'S FOR YOUR EXPENSES. C'YA"

She balled it up and added it to the shards of glass on the floor. One man had already tried to walk away from her. Phillip saw how that worked out. What made him think she wouldn't seek revenge on him?

Of course, winning Blake back was not an act of revenge. It was simply regaining what was rightfully hers. Time was a crucial factor now. What if Phillip let his buddy know he was gone? He'd still have to pay the rent to keep the apartment, wouldn't he? Could she get away with staying there? She could say she was a relative if the landlord knocked on the door. But she didn't know Phillip's friend's name. The rent was due in two-and-a-half weeks. Hopefully, she had at least that much time.

It was a small window to get rid of Noreen once and for all. She'd have to do it alone. Once that whore-nurse was out of the picture, Blake would take care of her. After all, she was the mother of his child.

She ran to the bedroom and searched under the bed where Phillip usually kicked his cameras and computer. Nothing. She rummaged through the lone bureau drawer he used. If he left her for good, he hadn't taken the measly pieces of clothing he wore. Maybe this was just a threat.

She slammed the drawer shut. Dammit. Phillip's laptop had Noreen's hospital schedule and habits on it. No matter. If Phillip was smart enough to follow her, so could she. Only she wouldn't merely watch Noreen walk into a grocery store, she'd plow into her. Do what he didn't have the nerve to. Accidents like that happen all the time in busy parking lots.

What was it Phillip said? He'd tracked Noreen shopping at the same market and usually after her shift ended in the morning before she went home. He'd mentioned that was one of the few times she seemed to be alone. He'd observed that someone always seemed to be with Noreen, as if she were incapable of performing simple tasks without a witness. Or a bodyguard.

His description had delighted Lynne at the time. They were right to fear her. And to try to protect Noreen.

That simple nurse friend of hers was practically glued to her side when Blake wasn't, Phillip had commented.

Well, two nurses for the price of one wasn't such a bad idea either. It would serve the woman right for befriending the whore-nurse.

She had to act fast. Thankfully, she still had one of Blake's credit cards. He'd opened the account solely for her in case she planned to buy something to surprise him, he explained shortly after they were married, Was it still active? She hadn't used it in over a year. Had he remembered it and closed it?

Without a car, she was crippled. If she couldn't rent one on this card, she'd have to enlist Fran's help. Fran had no life beyond Dalton House. She was one of those people starved for friendship who grasped the smallest show of interest and magnified it into a lifelong relationship. Within ten minutes of meeting her that first day in the rehabilitation house, she had Fran eating out of her hand just by acting helpless and desperate herself. The woman was far too invested in her for Lynne to feel comfortable. But she could be useful.

She pocketed the one-hundred-dollar bill and called a transportation service.

25

Joe burst through the door and Blake immediately had a déjà vu sensation to a week earlier when his entrance was equally as robust. Joe's words spilled from his mouth like Gia when she was overexcited about anything princess related.

His face even resembled his daughter's in her enthusiasm about whatever matter she was babbling. His eyes were wide, his cheeks flushed, and his words garbled.

"Lewey, I talked to him," Joe huffed. "What a dirt bag. He took money. I wish I'd had more on me. He told me her plans."

Blake couldn't contain his smile. It was rather cute to see. Just like watching his six-year-old.

"Take it easy, Joey." He reached for his coffee. "I thought you were off today. What are you doing here at the station?"

"I am off. But I knew you were here covering for Captain Warren. Listen, I talked to the man living with Lynne. The photographer. The janitor Noreen recognized at the hospital. She wasn't wrong about that. He's been dogging her for Lynne."

The coffee soured in Blake's stomach. "Wait. What?" He

shook his head to clear it. "Slow down, please. What are you talking about?"

Joe braced his hands on the back of the chair facing Blake. "He's one of Noreen's anonymous callers. He turned up at the hospital. I told you Kelly got hold of his employment records. I staked out the address he listed. Not the nicest part of town. It took almost twenty-four hours, but I saw him. Followed him to a local watering hole. The bartender treated him like a regular, which suits the guy because the place was a dump. Anyway, after a couple beers, he owned up that he's living with Lynne. More like she's living with him. He called her a lunatic with a hard-on for a nurse who works at Children's Hospital. He never mentioned Noreen by name so maybe he's a little bit smart. Said she insisted he get the janitor's job with some crazy scheme to cause "the nurse," Joe framed air quotations, "to have an accident. But he said she was hard to get to and he wasn't interested in getting himself in trouble."

Joe's words slammed into Blake's chest like a boxer's left jab. The force pushed him back against his chair. "Jesus."

Joe nodded. "He claims he's never been arrested and that might be true because he doesn't appear to have a criminal record. One of my cop friends ran his name."

Joe always seemed to know "a guy" who could do a favor and find information that wasn't supposed to be public. It amazed him. Joe kept talking.

"This piece of crap was almost depressed. Said he's dug himself into a hole he can't get out of and he didn't think twice when I offered to help. Once he started talking, there was no shutting him up. I was like his priest or something. He said Lynne talked about kidnapping Gia and taking her out of the country."

The boxer's second jab hit Blake square in the heart. His head jerked toward the analog clock on the wall. Thank God she was still in school. He'd be picking her up at the end of the day, working only half of Captain Warren's shift. But was she safe there?

He reached for his phone to call the school. "Where is this man now? What's his name?"

"I paid for a couple nights at that room-in-a-box motel. Rob's hanging around outside, out of sight, keeping an eye on him. Making sure he stays put. We talked long enough at the bar to make him late for work, but he didn't seem to mind. I suggested I'd make good on his lost wages."

He paused while Blake spoke to the school principal, requested a welfare check on his daughter, and tapped his pen double-time on the desk blotter waiting for a response.

"She is? Thank you. She's not to be released to anyone except me, do you understand? Not her mother or anyone who might claim to represent her mother. You're familiar with Gia's situation and some recent incidents are heightening our safety concerns. I'm the only one picking Gia up this afternoon. Tell me you understand."

He disconnected the call. "I don't give a damn about the school's image. I'm hiring private security for my daughter. I—"

Joe interrupted. "Hold on, Blake, there's more."

He held his breath. What could be worse?

"Kidnapping Gia was just one of Lynne's schemes. She's after Noreen."

A headache exploded in Blake's skull. "Tell me everything."

WHAT THE FUCK was he going to do now? Phillip scanned the motel room. The carpet was worn, the furniture warped and older than the stuff at the apartment, and the bathroom smelled a little like sewage. A lot of cable channels though. That was a plus.

This guy Joe was passing himself off as a bud, but he knew

better. No one outta the clear blue offers to put you up for a couple nights without an agenda. He'd gotten drunk and spent the night here on Joe's dime but now it was morning and his head was somewhat clearer.

Last night, he'd spilled his guts about Lynne and her crazy antics. It felt kinda good to unburden himself like that. Like getting everything off his chest allowed him to be innocent of it all. Not that he was guilty of much. There was no law against fucking a crazy woman.

The more he drank, the more he talked. And Old Joe sure was interested. He asked a lot of questions. The right questions. He kept saying he knew Lynne, knew how she operated. But it felt like something else, like he was fishing for information. Somewhere during the conversation, he didn't care anymore. It didn't matter that he missed his shift at the Hellspital. He ignored his supervisor's three phone calls.

He ignored Lynne's phone call too, even though Old Joe encouraged him to answer it. Lately, every phone call from her ended in a screaming match. He'd known she wouldn't be there when he sneaked back to the apartment to snatch the rest of his weed. Old Joe waited in the car. For a woman who was broke, she made sure she got her nails and hair done all the time.

He'd taken one last look around the dump and left a note. Old Joe had been right. It was time for something better.

His stomach growled and he lit the half smoked joint from last night. Where was he exactly? Old Joe had driven him here, ordered a pizza and bought beer, and assured him he'd return.

How far was he from the bar? Was his car still there? How would he get to it? He walked in his undershorts to the dresser and grabbed a cold slice. With the slice hanging from his mouth, he walked into the bathroom to pee. Even he couldn't drink beer this early. He needed coffee.

The handful of money Old Joe gave him to stay here was

wadded up beside the pizza box. How much was it? Enough to blow this pop stand? His stomach growled again. He sniffed the underarms of his shirt. Not too bad. Stepping into his jeans, he gathered the cash and found his shoes. First things first. Breakfast.

HE'D EATEN half of his meal when Old Joe showed up, grinning like they were best friends. Guess it wasn't too hard to find him since the diner was next to the motel.

"How ya doin' this morning?"

He stuffed his mouth full of pancake and eyed Old Joe. What was his real objective? Did Old Joe think he was stupid? "Whadda you want with me, man?"

Old Joe's head bobbed. "I want to keep that criminal record of yours clean. I want you to help me save a woman's life, maybe even a little girl's. I want you to do the right thing."

The right thing? Did he know what that was anymore? "Not sure what you mean."

"Yeah you are. You know Lynne Matthews is up to something. You know what she's capable of, abduction and arson. You said last night you were around for the fire that destroyed her house."

"I didn't have nothin' to do with that fire."

Joe nodded. "I know that's what you said and I believe you, man. But you and I both know Lynne could claim differently. Hell, she could blame the whole thing on you."

He'd worried about that. But it was last year and no one died. And they'd charged Lynne with the arson. They weren't likely still investigating it.

The waitress topped off his coffee. Old Joe waved her off without ordering anything. He longed for the rest of that joint back at the room.

"So what do you say, Phil? Help me avert whatever scheme Lynne Matthews is cooking up."

"I told you I don't know. She has so many crazy ideas, all boiling over like an overheated radiator. One day she wants something, the next something else. The woman is crazy. I ain't goin' back there."

"I'm not asking you to."

"Well then what do you want with me." Maybe if he spoke each word clearly, Old Joe would get the message.

"Go to the police with me."

"Hell no."

"Tell them everything you told me last night about Lynne Matthews. There could be a reward in it for you."

That grabbed his attention. "Could be or is? How much?"

"Enough for you to get away from here. Away from Lynne Matthews. Enough to make a fresh start somewhere."

He'd been thinking about a new start. Talked about it with his buds. There was nothing holding him here. Nothing left at the apartment that he couldn't leave. He slouched against the booth seat.

"How do I know this isn't a setup? The minute I go to the cops, they'll arrest me. I didn't have nothing to do with that nurse going missing, but she could lie and say I did. She could accuse me of a lot of shit. I'm not stupid enough to go looking for trouble."

Old Joe thought about that for a minute. "What if I can assure you no one will file any charges against you?"

"How you gonna do that? You can't."

Old Joe was between a rock and a hard spot now. He breathed heavy, like he was deflated. "Look man, you admit that Lynne Matthews is crazy. You said yourself she's determined to hurt the nurse, maybe even the little girl. You've been a party to those plans. That's called being an accomplice. Right now, you're balls deep in it. I know you were at the park when she met with Gia and the social service worker."

Fuck. How could he know that? He sat up straighter. The shirt started to smell now from his sweat.

Joe's voice rose. "I know you finagled your way into a birthday party and took more pictures of Noreen Jensen then the birthday girl. I know you're at the hospital solely to stalk Noreen Jensen." He reached for his phone and twisted it side to side. "You're not the only photographer here. I've got pictures of my own."

Holy shit. How'd Old Joe know all this? He could jump up from the table and bolt for the door. Out run Old Joe. But run where? Back to Lynne. Wasn't that the frying pan into the fire?

Old Joe sighed. "Look, man. I'm giving you a chance to get out of it and land on the right side of the law. Go to the police with me and I'll go to bat for you. But we do it now, today. There isn't going to be a second chance."

"Right now? Like right now?"

Old Joe nodded.

He still had some cash hidden in the storage unit at the apartment. He'd remembered it last night. "And there's a reward?"

Old Joe nodded again.

"If I go with you, I gotta make a stop first."

"I'll go with you."

Old Joe wasn't giving him any breathing room.

He wouldn't mind trying some place new. Maybe someplace warmer. Where it didn't snow. He'd said more than once he'd had enough of Lynne. Said it last night a hundred times. Even told that to her face. She hadn't believed him. His buddies had laughed at him, like he was some kind of loser with nowhere to go.

He eyed Old Joe. "Can you help me get outta town?"

"Yep."

With cash in his pocket, he could find a new Sugar Mama. Someone better than Lynne. She'd looked good in the beginning, but he'd ended up supporting her in the end. And putting up with a lot of crap. He wiped his mouth, balled up his napkin and dropped it on his dirty plate. Why the fuck not?

26

Noreen tossed her purse onto the passenger seat, slid into her car, and dragged the driver's door shut. Immediately she touched the lock button and the click of the latch raised goose bumps on her arms.

It was Blake's newest directive. He didn't want her to wait to start the engine, fasten her seatbelt, and shift into gear, automatically locking the car. Vulnerable seconds, he'd called them.

"Lock the door immediately, please," he'd pleaded. "And then take the gun out of the glove box and keep it within reach."

Until Blake came home that day with the handgun, she hadn't really considered the consequences of carrying a concealed weapon. He was right, guns in the right hands were nothing to be afraid of. She'd never contemplated holding one in her own hands.

She resisted at first but couldn't argue with Blake's logic that it offered security, protection and, if necessary, a dependable defense.

A friend of Blake's operated a firing academy and she enrolled in a handgun safety course. She surprised herself with her accuracy firing at the target of a body outline and easily certified.

She removed the weapon from the dashboard compartment. Having it with her now was like making sure she had her wallet. The hospital was the only place she didn't carry it. Weapons weren't permitted on the premises.

Kelly had surprised her with the admission that she was an accomplished shot and also owned a pistol. They joked about the cop shows where the actors shoved their guns in their pants and speculated how it never fell out their pant legs. But this was no joking matter. Kelly was happy she learned to shoot.

The black Smith & Wesson lay flat in her palm. Only six inches long. It weighed a little over a pound but felt heavier in her hand. Perhaps that was because of the circumstances related to its existence.

During training, the sound of the nine-millimeter bullet leaving the chamber was so crisp, she felt it. Like a dog bite. Or frigid winter temperatures that pinched her face. The trigger was a clean pull, according to her instructor. That was some of the lingo she'd picked up at the range. He'd praised her ability to place the bullet right where he directed. The heart. The forehead. An eye.

The corners of her mouth dipped low into a frown. She'd never shoot anything real with it.

She slipped it into the outside pocket of her bag. Damn, where was the grocery list? Still on the kitchen counter? Last night's shift had been busy with two emergencies that practically drained her. Her leg hurt. Her back was tired. She longed for a hot shower and a couple solid hours of sleep.

She turned the key in the ignition, mentally visualizing the lilac-colored Things To Do tablet that she kept in the corner of the kitchen counter and added groceries to as necessary. Milk was written on it, and Gia's favorite rainbow cereal. What else? The list had at least six items, she was sure. But those were the only two her mind's eye saw. Oh well. She'd grabbed those along with fresh fruit and if necessary, make another trip to the supermarket later. Or again tomorrow after work.

The nearest parking space to the store's front entry was available and she slipped her car into it, grateful that at least one thing was going her way.

A small red car seemed to follow her the four blocks from the hospital and now it drove past her parking space. The bright morning sun obliterated her vision, making it impossible for her to see inside. Probably some other tired nurse stopping at the market on her way home.

Blake had instilled such a strong sense of awareness of her surroundings in her that she noticed things now she'd never been attentive to before. Like the clothes that lone man leaning against the pole wore, with his shirt buttoned to its collar even though it was already warm this morning, and the lack of running shoes on the couple jogging toward the entrance. Like license plates. She squinted but couldn't catch the red car's numbers in the sun's glare.

Walking into the store, her head swiveled. Few customers shopped at this hour. Nevertheless, the air was charged with a nervous energy and Noreen tensed her shoulders as she retrieved a shopping basket. She could walk every aisle to jar her memory of the items on the list, but today didn't feel like the day to do that. For whatever reason, the store was giving her the creeps. Looking over her right shoulder and then her left, there was no reason for the trepidation. She probably was just overtired.

She hurried to the dairy aisle and then snatched a family-sized box from the cereal shelf. The urge to rush home moved her feet faster. Self-checkout was empty and she breezed through, ripping the plastic bag and its contents from the metal holder. She ran to her car, uttering a second appreciation that it was parked so close to the front entrance, tossed the bag into the passenger seat, fell into her seat, and dragged the door closed. She punched the lock button and gulped. The fear was so palpable, she was perspiring. She started the car and hiked up the air.

Deep, controlled breaths would calm her. Eyes closed, she made a conscious effort to fill her lungs to capacity and expel the air slowly, blowing it out her mouth. She repeated the exercise, and her pulse slowed. Opening her eyes, her focus on the rearview mirror caught the red car cruising past her spot again. Was she in someone's parking space? It was more than a coincidence that the car was stalking her.

Again, she hadn't noticed the driver. Couldn't tell if it was a man or a woman. Nevertheless, the hairs on the back of her neck prickled. Starting the car, she backed out of the space and held her breath until she turned down her street. She crossed her fingers that Blake might already be home from taking Gia to school. She needed his arms around her more than a cup of coffee.

He waited for her in the kitchen. Without kicking off her shoes or dropping her purse, she rushed into his embrace. He crushed her closer.

"Hey! What happened? You're shaking like a leaf. What's the matter?"

Her face remained buried in his chest. "I... I'm not sure. Nothing. I just got spooked."

Blake's hands spread wide and he rubbed small circles into her back. "Shh, you're home now. What scared you? Sweetheart, talk to me." He gently eased her back to see her face, just as he'd done a thousand times when Gia was frightened.

She wiped her runny nose with the back of her hand, then stepped out of his arms. Moving to the kitchen table, she unloaded her purse and toed off her shoes. "Goodness, Blake, I left groceries in the car."

"I'll get them in a minute. Tell me what happened."

What did happen? Her overtired, overactive imagination got the best of her "Nothing, not really. I had a weird sensation in the grocery store. There was barely anyone in there. I thought a red car was following me. At least I think it was the same red car I saw every time." Her thumb and fingers pressed into the back of her neck, where a dull ache thumped. "We had a terrible night on the floor last night. We almost lost a two-year-old."

"I'm sorry. What about the car? Did you see the driver? Get a license plate?"

Her fingers relocated to the bridge of her nose and she pinched. Blake's concern was endearing but her nerves were frayed.

"I'm really tired this morning. I may have simply overreacted. I'm on edge. We were all stressed and in the middle of the emergency, Kelly felt ill." Blake's eyebrows rose. "She became lightheaded. Her doctor is still trying to regulate her blood pressure and it dropped so low, she almost fainted. We sent her home early."

Anticipating his question, she added, "Her boyfriend came for her. But I'm worried about her and finishing the night short-handed seems to have gotten the best of me." She pressed her fingers to her forehead. "I'm going to get some sleep. As I think about it, I'm not sure it wasn't just a shopper driving in behind me."

Blake came up to her, his head canted in doubt.

She pressed her hands against his chest. "Honest. All your warnings and cautions have jumbled together in my head and I panicked. It's fine. Did you get Gia off to school all right? Did you speak to the principal about the security guard?"

Blake poured a cup of coffee for her. "I don't mean to make you crazy with all my advisories. I only want you to be aware. Yes, we now have private security keeping an eye on Gia while she's in school and I feel much better. The company sent a young woman who looks like she's sixteen years old. I had to ask her for identification because I didn't believe she was credentialed. Wait until you meet her. Her name is Lana. She wore blue jeans and sneakers and has a bright purple streak in long, dark hair. She looks like a student herself. She's posing as a student teacher, logging hours monitoring the class. Neither Gia nor any of her classmates know any differently. Only Gia's teacher and the principal. Her teacher, I trust. The principal, I'm not so wild about. He's not on board with the idea but I threatened him with legal action and a public outcry, and he conceded. Temporarily, he made sure to stress. It wasn't a pleasant conversation but at least we have a sentry in place."

Noreen took a deep breath. "That's a relief."

He squeezed her shoulders. "There's something else, rather someone else, I need to talk to you about. A guy—"

Simultaneously, their phones rang. Noreen groaned, seeing it was the hospital and Blake went in search of his, heading toward the dining room. He was still engaged in conversation when she penned a note and laid it on his laptop. "If you wanna have a naked lunch date with me, wake me up in a couple hours. We'll talk then. I love you." He grinned and she headed toward the bedroom.

27

Her dreams made restful sleep impossible. The red car followed her everywhere. To work. To the grocery store. Into the bathroom to shower. Noreen awoke about an hour later in a cold sweat, foggy, and still tired. But sleep was too elusive.

She switched her phone out of Do Not Disturb mode and saw one missed call and one text from Kelly asking her to call. She dialed her friend.

"Girl, I'm sorry to bother you 'cause I know you're probably trying to get some sleep. But Adam can't miss work and the damn doctor says I can't be home alone. May I come over and camp out at your house? I'm not doing anything but lying on the couch anyway watching terrible TV and dozing."

Noreen tsked. "You're not supposed to drive, remember? I'll come to your place. Do you need anything? I can pick up groceries or whatever."

"Is Blake home? Did you two have plans? Something romantic and sexy and I'm messing everything up?"

"No real plans. Don't worry about that. I didn't get much sleep. A red car really spooked me. I thought it was following me. I'm still not sure. I'll tell you about it when I come over. I can nap in that oversized recliner that I love. We can be lazy together."

"Okay. Thanks, you're a good friend. I could use some cranberry juice if you want to stop at the convenience store at the corner. I'm supposed to stay hydrated and I can't drink one more drop of plain water. The juice at least makes it palatable."

"Got it. See you shortly."

Blake offered to accompany her to Kelly's and spend the afternoon with "his ladies." The reference made her smile, knowing that the man she loved and her best friend loved each other. How lucky was she?

She eyed the stack of files and open notebook on the dining room table. "Wouldn't you rather stay here and map out some new rescue procedure or training program? It sure looks like that's what you had on your agenda."

He nodded. "It's due soon and I couldn't finish it at the station. I thought I could do it here. I'll only need a couple hours. I'll call and check on the two of you later and maybe bring over takeout. But listen, I want you to be extra cautious. Joe has a guy under wraps who's been conspiring with Lynne." Her forehead tightened when her eyebrows furrowed. "I haven't talked to him yet. Joe says he seems harmless but I want to sit down with him myself. He's been following you and he says Lynne had some crazy scheme to kidnap Gia."

Her skin prickled with goosebumps. "My God, Blake. I think I saw him at the hospital."

Blake nodded. "He's been working there. But not anymore. He—when did you see him? You didn't tell me."

"I meant to but the time never seemed right. And it will take too long now. I should get to Kelly's."

"Promise you'll be careful. I'll come over as soon as I finish this and we can discuss it. I'll get it done much faster if I'm here alone." He drew her into his arms. "With you here I probably wouldn't be able to concentrate anyway." His hand dropped to her bottom. "I'd be thinking of other things."

His lips, as always, ignited a flame deep in her core and heated her heart. Breathless, she stepped out of his embrace, chuckled, and blew him a kiss as she exited the room.

"Get to work but keep a good thought, Lewey."

~

CONCENTRATION WAS DIFFICULT. Blake outlined the same four-step rescue policy three times before shoving the legal pad aside and tossing his pen to the table. He couldn't get Joe's words out of his head. Had Lynne really thought she could kidnap Gia and take her to another country? It was mind-boggling.

She couldn't possibly carry out such a plan, could she? How? She didn't have a passport to his knowledge. Where would she get the money to travel? From this unknown man Joe had tracked down? Who was he? Where had she met him? In the rehabilitation home? Before that?

Had he been an overlooked accomplice to the events of last year?

At least Joe had him squirreled away. But for how long?

He'd feel better if he talked to the man himself. He appeared young in the photos from the park. What'd he want with Lynne, an older woman with literally nothing to offer? What was in it for him? He could grill the kid for hours with the thousand questions that stormed his mind.

Joe didn't answer his phone, so he called Gia's school. Since his lunch in Noreen's arms wasn't going to happen, he'd spend time with the other lady who lit up his life. From the school, he could go to wherever Joe had deposited Lynne's friend and interrogate him.

Odd. No one answered at the school. He dialed a second

time. Still no answer. It was eleven-fifteen. Lunch was starting. Surely someone was in the office. When the third ring went unanswered, he ran to his truck.

Speeding toward Gia's school, he snapped on the fire radio. Units were on the way there for a reported bomb threat. Evacuation procedures were underway. But he knew better. This was a diversionary tactic intended to create chaos. This was an emergency designed to get to Gia.

He floored the gas pedal. There was little comfort knowing that Gia's personal security guard was in the building. What if he'd been duped? What if she was working with Lynne too? Lynne could have a host of predators she met in rehab just waiting to get their hands on his little girl.

He slammed his hand against the steering wheel. The background check he ran on the guard was thorough. But what if he missed something?

His truck screeched to a halt behind a police car blocking traffic from driving too near the building. He jumped out and ran the distance. Students were everywhere, laughing, yelling, crying, but for the most part corralled into groups. He searched for Gia's teacher without finding her. He didn't recognize any of the little faces of Gia's classmates. Where the hell were they? Held hostage inside?

His heart smashed against his chest so forcefully, he fought to breathe. He ran to the nearest uniform and flashed his badge.

"Lieutenant Matthews. Deep Creek Twelve. Is everyone out of the building? My daughter is missing. I don't see her anywhere."

The police officer eyed his badge, lifted his radio to his mouth, and called for a situation report. Three separate checkpoints reported the building was empty. None had found a device that could be an explosive, but their grid search wasn't complete.

Blake ran his fingers through his hair and surveyed the sea of tiny blond and bobbing brunette heads. Where was Argia? Where was the bodyguard? At the request of the police officer, he ducked back under the yellow caution tape that cordoned off the perimeter of the school and joined the crowd of onlookers and worried parents behind the line. He stood at attention when he saw two security vans arrive on the scene and park fender to fender across the road to form a roadblock. It was the private company he hired to protect Gia.

He darted toward one of the drivers, a burly man taller than him. Breathless, he introduced himself. "I'm Blake Matthews. You're hired to protect my daughter. What's happened? What are you doing here?"

The seconds it took for the man to respond felt like hours. The driver extended his hand and introduced himself. "Relax, Mr. Matthews. Everything is under control. Lana contacted us per procedure the minute she sensed unexpected activity. It's standard operating procedure for our company. We're here simply as back up. She should be..." he scrolled on his phone and then pivoted, "right over there." Blake followed his gaze to a four-dour silver sedan. Gia's bodyguard stepped out of the driver's seat, walked around the rear of the car, and opened the back door. Two rainbow sneakers touched the asphalt.

"Daddy!"

His knees weakened with relief and he dropped to the ground. Gia ran toward him, with Lana less than a foot behind, Gia's puppy backpack flapping from her hand. Gia flew into his outstretched arms. "Hi, Daddy."

"She's fine, sir. A real trooper."

A hint of vanilla wafted from the luxurious chestnut curls that covered his face. Noreen had allowed Gia to use some of her shampoo last night. That aroma combined with the arms around his neck grounded him again.

He stood, lifting Gia with him. "What happened?"

Lana pursed her lips and shook her head. "I'm not certain, sir. I didn't like the situation. Gia's teacher confirmed a fire drill wasn't scheduled. She seemed surprised and that didn't sit right with me. That's why I called our office. I thought it best to isolate your daughter until we could assess the veracity of the drill."

She smiled. "You've raised a heck of a little girl. She didn't want to come with me. Said I was a stranger. Said her daddy taught her never to go with someone she didn't know. Even though her teacher reassured her it was okay, she hesitated."

"Daddy, she has a badge. Just like you."

He swallowed the lump in his throat. "She does? How do you know that?"

"She showed me. Is she your friend, Daddy? She said so."

He felt giddy with relief. "Yes, Peanut, she's our friend."

"She wanted me to sit in the front but I told her I'm too little." He laughed, reached for his vibrating cell phone, and froze.

A text from Noreen.

He placed Gia on her feet. "You stay with Lana, okay? Will you follow me? And you gentlemen too? We've got trouble."

28

D riving the back roads, Kelly's home was about fifteen minutes away, even though they lived in different towns. At first, Noreen didn't give the red car behind her a second thought. There were thousands of red cars out there. Until she turned right into the mini mart and it did too. She circled the store twice, cruising until one of the spots directly in front of the automatic sliding glass door opened.

While she waited for the gentleman to get settled and evacuate the premium parking space, the red car rolled past. The click of her left turn blinker mimicked her racing heart while she studied her hunter. It was the same car as earlier today.

It idled at the far corner. The driver hunched low in the seat wearing a ball cap and sunglasses. This was no coincidence.

Several thoughts ran through her mind. Back out of the spot and drive straight to the police station. Except she was unsure where the Penn Hills station was located and how far it might be. Too dangerous to be on the road. What if this was the driver who forced her and Kelly off the road weeks earlier?

Drive straight to Kelly's. Her house was about one-hundred-and-fifty yards down the street. And bring danger to her doorstep? She dismissed that thought immediately. Drive back home to Blake.

What if the driver didn't know where they lived? She'd be leading them right to their driveway. That wasn't a good plan either.

She unfastened her seatbelt and reached for her purse. The weight of her bag assured her that the pistol was tucked inside. Still, she checked it. Locked and loaded. She'd be safer inside the store, and from there, she'd call the police.

Giving the car one last glance, she opened the driver's door and hustled inside the store. Two customers waited to check out, the woman in front chatting happily with the young girl behind the counter.

"Excuse me." All eyes turned toward her. "I'm sorry to interrupt. I think I'm being followed. I'm going to call the police. May I wait here?"

The store employee's eyes widened, and she nodded. The man in line behind the woman puffed out his chest and strode to the front door. She guessed he was in his forties, a little flabby but by no means weak. "You in some kind of trouble, ma'am? Who do you say is following you?" He stepped through the entry into the sunshine and shaded his eyes with his hand.

She punched 9-1-1 and waited for the connection. The gentleman pointed to the red car. "Is that them? Over there?"

She reached the door in time to watch the red car whiz by. It passed too fast. She didn't see the license plate.

Her voice was an octave higher than usual. "Did you see a driver? Did you catch the plate number?" The gentleman walked back inside.

"Nope. There wasn't a plate on that car. Coulda been removed. Or it could be a car dealer. You want me to wait here with you for the police?"

She'd forgotten she'd dialed the emergency number. She apologized to the operator for a misunderstanding and hung up. What would she tell them? An unknown driver with an unknown license plate in a red car she saw earlier was following her but left, perhaps because it wasn't actually following her? It would be just like the phone call to the police about the dead flowers. She had no real information to tell them. She was on her own to figure it out.

"Did you see what make of car it was?"

The man mumbled. "Sorry, I'm out of touch with these newer models. I think it was American made, maybe a Chevy or a Ford. Not sure. Looked like there was a paper in the window, like a rental. But I was trying to see the driver. You okay? Want me to follow you somewhere?"

Damn. No concrete details to tell Blake either. As soon as she was safely at Kelly's, she'd call him. She didn't want to discuss it in this public atmosphere. She texted instead. *Think I'm being followed. The red car again. Will call from Kelly's. Can you come?*

"Ma'am? Want me to follow you?"

"No, no thank you. I'll be fine. My friend lives at the end of this street. Thanks for the offer, though. I think you scared them away. I appreciate it."

He reached for his wallet to pay for his items, still sitting by the cash register. The cashier acted as if something like this happened every day, snapping her gum, and ringing up the purchases without a second glance at Noreen. "No problem. You take care, ma'am."

The cashier didn't seem to notice her trembling hands when she paid for two half-gallons of cranberry juice. Clutching the bag in one hand and keeping her other on the handgun inside her unzipped purse, Noreen returned to her car. Sweaty hands gripped the steering wheel when she eased back and drove out of the parking lot.

Kelly's house sat on the right side of the dead end street. Noreen always drove to the undeveloped lot that blocked further progress of the road, turned around and parked across from Kelly's front porch. That way, her car faced the direction she needed to go when she left.

At the corner stop sign, she looked left and then right and proceeded through the intersection. The red car followed. Where had it come from? Crawling at five miles per hour, she narrowed her eyes to hone in on the rearview mirror. Who the hell was driving?

She removed her phone from the cup holder and hit the call button. Kelly's phone displayed as the last number called. She pressed the button and prayed her friend wasn't asleep.

"Hey Girlfriend."

She didn't mean to yell, but she did. "Call 9-1-1 right away. I'm here. So is the red car that's been following me. Call now!"

Her options were limited. Turn into Kelly's driveway, and essentially be blocked in if the red car stopped at the end. Or drive to the end of the street and turn back to face this bastard.

Enough was enough. Time to find out who terrorized her. And stop it.

She rode to the end of the street, turned around in the dirt patch that bordered the open field, and stopped. The red car maneuvered to block her exit, waiting several car lengths away and parking horizontally across the roadway. The car engine revved.

How far away was Blake? Or the police. She sent a second text to Blake. *red car. Kelly's. NOW!*

Home was fifteen minutes away and knowing him, he'd cut that travel time to ten.

She eyed the red car. The driver hadn't stepped out of the car, hadn't rolled down the window to communicate, hadn't moved.

Was it Lynne? Whose car did she drive? Blake had mentioned she didn't have a vehicle and he'd sold the SUV she drove when they were married. That had been a screaming match she was happy to miss.

Should she wait for the police and Blake? Just sit here at the mercy of this demon? That seemed dumb. And left her vulnerable.

She'd watched too many crime shows with Blake not to realize that if she stepped out of the car from the driver's side, she presented a full view of herself to this creep.

Kicking off her peep toe pumps, she threw her right leg over the console, contorted to raise herself up and over it, and dragged her left leg with her to plop in the passenger seat. She dragged her purse onto her lap and slipped the strap across her body. Its weight pressed into her thigh reassuringly.

Despite the air conditioning running, sweat pooled along her back. Her mouth was desert dry. There'd been a bottle of water in the second cup holder, but she tossed everything into the back seat to climb over the console. It lay on the floor, out of reach.

In her peripheral vision, the red blur moved. The car changed its position, rolling back and forth, back and forth until its headlights faced her again, head on. And then, as if watching a horror movie, the sun bounced off the shiny chrome bumper and created a starburst of light as the car zoomed toward her.

Noreen smashed her purse against her belly with her left hand, clutched the door handle with her right and threw her shoulder against the panel. She fell out of the passenger seat and rolled into the field, eating mud and weeds and bugs.

The sound was ear splitting when the car crashed into her brand new SUV. Tires squealed and the smell of burning rubber filled the air. Metal crunched in a spine tingling wail, like nails on a chalkboard amplified a thousand times.

The impact shoved the mangled debris toward Noreen, a giant mound of steel and fiberglass closing in on her. She screamed and hunched up on all fours, clawing at the earth, hustling backward and toward the left, anticipating what path the oncoming ball of metal might take and praying she was stumbling out of its way. Dirt clogged her mouth and tears stung her eyes. Her chest heaved watching the wreckage steamroll toward her and then veer off to the right. Sliding from the asphalt into the field at such a high speed imbedded the red car's front tires in the dirt, impeding further progress. The red car bounced off hers like a ping pong ball.

The airbags inflated in both vehicles and a loud maniacal scream echoed from the red car. A woman's scream.

Smoke wafted from the engines of both vehicles and the odor of oil and gasoline gagged Noreen. She jammed her eyes closed and fought the memories of the smell, the fear of fire. Her leg wasn't broken. She wasn't locked in a cellar. But was she fighting for her life again? Was she strong enough?

Still on her hands and knees, her vision blurred, she narrowed her eyes and watched horrified as the driver's door of the red car creaked open.

First one sandaled foot and then a second dropped to the ground. Dirty blond hair lifted in the breeze when Lynne stepped out of the car, floating around her face like spider webs. She clung to the doorframe with two hands and looked around wildly. Blood dripped from her nose. She stepped unsteadily to open the backdoor and lean inside.

Neighbors poured out of their houses, running toward the wreckage. Noreen saw Kelly, her eyes wide, her mouth moving but the words she yelled blown away on the wind.

Lynne hobbled toward her mangled SUV, dragging her right foot at an odd angle. She braced herself against what was now merely a shiny white heap of junk and peered into the driver's seat.

Noreen compressed herself to the ground. Sirens blared in the distance. Blake had to be close.

Lynne's yell was shrill. "Where are you bitch? You can't hide from me. You better come out if you want to see Argia alive. Do you hear me?" Her head pivoted wildly searching for her.

Argia? Did she say Argia? The commotion of neighbors yelling, her ears ringing, and Lynne's incoherent rants combined to confuse her.

Lynne raised her arms in the air like a referee signaling a touchdown. That's when she saw the rifle. The barrel pointed toward the sky. Dear Lord, did she know how to use it? It would stand to reason that if Blake had encouraged her to learn to shoot, he might have trained Lynne too.

Her muscles constricted to shrink her size. Her chin sunk into the mud.

Lynne whirled around and aimed the weapon at the approaching neighbors. "Stop!" The gun waved erratically at the crowd. "Everyone stay back. The first one of you who comes near me, I'll shoot. This is between me and that whore-nurse."

As if choreographed, the dozen or so residents took a step backward. Everyone except Kelly, who continued to advance toward Lynne as if walking on eggshells, her hands raised in surrender. Had she thought to grab her weapon? Was it tucked in her back waistband? Could Kelly see her hiding in the brush?

"Lynne?" Kelly's voice rose with concern. "That was a terrible crash. Are you hurt? Do you need my help?"

Atta girl, Kelly, play to her need for attention.

"Lynne? Can you hear me? No one cares what happened to Noreen, we're worried about you. We rushed out here to make sure you're all right. I already called for an ambulance."

What was the look on Lynne's face? Was it working?

Lynne aimed the rifle at Kelly's midsection and Noreen gasped.

"Stop right there." Kelly did.

The sirens were louder now. Nearer.

"Listen, Lynne, those sirens are for you. Every—"

The sound of the gunshot was deafening. People screamed and scattered, some ducking behind parked cars, others bolting between the houses. A windshield shattered. Kelly shrieked and dropped to the pavement. Noreen tasted bile in the back of her throat. Was Kelly hit?

Lynne howled her name like a crazed hyena.

"Norrreeeeen?" Her voice was octaves higher than normal. "Where are you? Look what you made me do. Your friend is hurt. You better come tend to her. And if you ever want to see Argia again, you'll come out now." She pivoted in a half circle, her arms flailing the air. "Don't make me shoot someone else. Come out now."

A sob escaped Noreen. She clamped her hand over her mouth to stifle any further noise. Was Kelly shot? She lay prone on the sidewalk, not moving. Gia was safe in school, wasn't she? Blake said this morning they had security in place. Had Lynne somehow managed to manipulate the guard? Blake said she was young. Maybe she was inexperienced.

Another rifle shot split the air. "Wheeeerrreee are yooooouuuu?"

A police car came to a screeching halt, the siren shutting off mid-blare. An officer ducked behind his open driver's door, his gun pointed at Lynne. "Ma'am drop the weapon. Drop it now."

Lynne ignored him. She lay behind Lynne in the direct path of the cop's aim. If he didn't see her and fired, he could miss Lynne altogether and shoot her. She raised up on both knees, palms in the air, and yelled.

"Don't shoot, officer. Please. She may have my daughter hidden somewhere. Don't hurt her."

Lynne twisted around to face Noreen, her features hideously knotted, her nostrils flaring, her eyes bulging. Immediately she recalled the hideous Halloween-like mask Lynne's face had contorted into that day in the dark cellar when dirt covered her face, blood ran from her nose and outlined her teeth. In the daylight, this was more horrifying. But this was a showdown long overdue.

Her words enraged Lynne. "*Your* daughter? How dare you? Who the hell do you think you are? You have nothing to do with her. She belongs to me. Blake belongs to me. I—"

From somewhere behind her, Blake's deep voice resonated through a bullhorn. "Lynne? It's Blake. Listen to me. Your fight is with me, not Noreen. Leave her alone. Maybe we can sit down and talk. Maybe we can work this out. You're Gia's mother. Mothers are important. If you hurt Noreen, you won't get the chance to be in Gia's life. But you have to put the rifle down first. Put the gun down now, Lynne."

Noreen scanned the cars, the street, the porches. Where was he? Her gaze landed on Kelly, belly crawling to safety beside a parked car. Thank God she was alive. The police officer stood at his opened door, his gun still clutched in both hands but pointed upward. "Listen to him, ma'am. Drop your weapon now."

"C'mon, Lynne." Blake was reasoning with her again. "Don't do this. No one has to get hurt today. You don't want Gia to see this. You don't want her to get hurt in the crossfire."

Where was Blake? And where was Argia?

Lynne apparently didn't hear any of it. She advanced on Noreen, limping. She must have injured her leg in the crash. That would be an irony to enjoy later.

She focused on the rifle, swinging loosely in Lynne's hand. Her training at the shooting range included time in the classroom, working from a textbook, learning to identify different types of weapons as well as signs of aggression displayed by an active shooter.

It wasn't the look on Lynne's face she needed to see. It was her hands. As long as her fingers didn't wrap around the trigger, as long as her arms remained slack, she wouldn't shoot.

But that could change in a split second. Her eyes watered at she stared at Lynne's hands. Lynne continued to hobble toward her. Blake tried again.

"Stop, Lynne. Maybe we can fix this before it gets out of hand. Lower the rifle, Lynne."

Lynne's wild eyes leveled on her. "Stand up, you little whore. Stand up so I can see you better." Her clothes were disheveled, her makeup smeared. Mascara smudged one eye into a black circle.

Noreen slid her purse from her hip to her stomach and dropped her hand inside. She stayed on her knees. Could Lynne see her clearly through the tall weeds. It didn't seem so.

"Where's Argia, Lynne?" Lynne searched the area looking for the spot her voice came from. "What have you done with her?"

Lynne sneered. "You don't care about Argia. You ruined everything. I had a good life until you came along. Now, I have nothing. You should have died in that fire. That was my plan. I was going to rescue Argia and tell everyone you were the one who meant her harm. I would've been the hero. A mother risking her life to save her daughter. But you spoiled it all. You were supposed to die there. But you're going to die now. I'm going to kill you."

The muscles in her arms flexed. Her fingers tightened on the rifle grip.

Behind Lynne, the officer stepped out from the behind the cruiser door, his gun aimed. "Drop the rifle. Now!"

Footfalls sounded on the asphalt and over Lynne's shoulder, Blake ran toward them. "Lynne! Don't!" Panic etched his face, his features distorted as if he ran at Mach Two speed.

A woman screamed. A man cussed. Kelly screamed her name. The commotion swirled around the two of them like a vortex, ringing in her ears, clogging her brain. Lynne dropped her head back and screeched. "It's all over now. They're mine now."

The rifle lifted to waist level and her forefinger slid onto the trigger.

Noreen gripped the handgun in her purse, her finger moving on the trigger as if synchronized with Lynne's.

Lynne lifted the rifle higher, aiming it at her head. Lynne's face had lost the look of a human. She shrieked something incoherent.

Her instructor's voice echoed in her head. "Take a breath. Both eyes open. Don't pull on the trigger. Squeeze."

No time to remove the weapon from her bag. No time to try to reason with her anymore. Lynne was beyond insane. She rotated her purse toward Lynne and squeezed.

29

The bullet ripped through Lynne's chest. The impact knocked her backward, the rifle in her right hand flying upward, discharging a single round. Her feet lifted off the ground and her cheeks puffed out with the whoosh of air that exploded from her lungs.

She dropped to the ground with a thud, her eyes as round as cantaloupes, blood trickling from her bright red lips.

Noreen bent to the weeds and vomited.

The best instructor in the world might train you how to shoot but he didn't teach you what to do afterward. How to watch the life gush out of the bullet hole you just fired into someone's chest. How to handle the stinging in your hand. The adrenaline rushing through your body. The simultaneous pounding of your heart and your head. Was she dead?

She burst into tears.

Blake fell to his knees beside her. "Noreen. My God, Noreen. Are you hit?" His hands lifted her face to his and he inspected it. "Speak to me. Are you hurt?"

The police officer kicked the rifle away from Lynne's limp hand and knelt over her. Was she dead?

Wrenching sobs shook Noreen. Her chest clutched. She couldn't breathe.

Kelly ran toward them and dropped to the ground next to the police officer. She leaned over Lynne, her nurse's training jumping into action. Neighbors gathered around her lifeless form, looks of horror on their faces, their hands pressed to their mouths, a man making the sign of the cross, a woman crying. Was she dead?

Blake shook her. His hands rolled down her sides, up her back. "Are you hurt? Noreen. Look at me. Look at me!"

His gray eyes pierced through the confusion, his gaze a straight line to clear thinking. Her chest heaved. Her whole body shook, to include her teeth knocking against each other. She stared back at him, unable to control her quivering chin. "Where's Argia?"

His brow furrowed.

"Argia. Where is she? She said I'd never see her again. Is she at school? Please check, check right now." Her fingers dug into Blake's biceps. "Call the school, Blake. Call now."

"It's okay. Argia's here. She's in the car over there with Lana. Relax, she's fine."

Here? In what car? She stared past Kelly and the policeman, scanning the growing cluster of bystanders. "Where?"

Blake squeezed her arms. "Are you hurt? I don't think you're shot but does anything hurt? Anything broken? Can you stand?"

She pressed his biceps equally as hard. "Where? Where's Gia?"

He stood, lifting her with him. "There. See that silver sedan? She's in that car. I hope to God she's still in the back seat. I was at the school when I got your text."

She squinted to focus. More sirens arrived and paramedics rushed to where Kelly and the police officer now stood beside Lynne.

"Blake? Is she dead?"

As if sensing her stare, Kelly looked at her and nodded slowly.

Bile rose in her throat again and she yanked from Blake's grip, took two steps away from him, bent at the waist, and threw up again. His strong hands grasped her shoulders and helped her stand. "You're all right, sweetheart. It's going to be okay."

Her bare feet sunk into the dirt. The dry grass nipped at her ankles. She hugged his chest and wept. A nurse takes an oath to do no harm. What had she done?

The paramedics prepared the gurney for Lynne's sheet-covered body as Blake nudged her to pass it, instructing her not to look. She stepped gingerly from the field to the sidewalk. Like the Red Sea parting, Kelly's neighbors opened a path for her and at the end of it, her best friend waited with arms wide, enfolding her in a bear hug.

"Oh my God, Kelly, I thought she shot you. I was so afraid."

Blake squeezed her shoulder. "Hang onto her, Kell, I'm going to check on Gia."

At the look of surprise on Kelly's face, he nodded in the direction of Lana's car. "She's over there. I'm praying she didn't watch any of this. I'm certain she heard the gunfire. She must be out of her mind scared. I'll be right back." Noreen sobbed harder.

Kelly rocked her like a baby. "I'm fine. Just a couple scrapes on my legs. We were all scared. You did good, girl." She kissed the top of her head. "It's okay. It's all over now."

She raised her gaze to see her friend's face. "Kelly, I shot her. I killed someone."

Kelly's brows shot upward. "No you didn't. You saved my life and every one of my neighbors who ran outside. You saved your own life. You saved your family. I'm so proud of you. If shooting that monster was the only way to do it then you did the right thing, child. Don't look at it any other way."

Kelly tightened her embrace and chuckled. "When this is all over, we're going shopping."

What a time to think about something like that. Noreen stepped back, her brows knitted.

"You're gonna need a new purse."

LANA STOOD beside the rear passenger door. Gia sat on the floor in the back seat of Lana's car, her feet pulled up to her chest with Mr. Fox and Mr. Dog balanced on each knee.

"I kept her inside, sir. I don't think she saw anything, but she heard everything."

How much more trauma could his baby girl handle? He opened the back door and slid in. "Hey, Peanut. What are you doing?"

She turned tear-rimmed eyes to him and whispered, "Is Mother still here?"

His heart splintered. He patted the seat. "Can you come up here and sit with me?"

She shook her head. "We have to hide, Daddy. Mother is looking for us. She's gonna hurt us again, me and Weenie."

That was a horror neither one of the women he loved would have to face again. "I'm too big to squish down there with you. Please come up here and sit beside me. I need to talk to you."

She waited so long, he didn't think she would. But she crawled into his lap and nestled her stuffed animals against his chest. Her tiny body shook. "Your mother isn't going to hurt you. Not anymore."

Her wide eyes were clear. "Did she hurt Weenie?"

By the grace of God, no. "No, Noreen is okay."

"Is she here?"

He looked through the windshield. Kelly still had her arm

around Noreen while two police officers appeared to be questioning her. He should be beside her but the gurney with Lynne's body remained in the field. What were they waiting for?

"She's here, honey, but she's busy talking to some people."

"Did she save us, Daddy?"

His head ached, his mouth was dry, he smelled of sweat and fear and he likely looked like hell. But he grinned.

"Yes, Gia, she did. Noreen saved us."

B lake and Noreen both rose when their attorney strode into his office, his smile confidant.

He shook Blake's hand, took Noreen's in his right hand, and covered it with his left.

"This proceeding is just a formality, Noreen. You needn't be concerned."

How could she not be? Fran Francis, the Dalton House counselor who'd befriended Lynne, claimed she could prove that Lynne's death was murder. She alleged that Noreen Jensen killed her to cover up for the house fire she started last year, in which Lynne was supposed to perish. She claimed that Noreen had tormented Lynne and stalked her in an attempt to eliminate Lynne from the picture and win Blake Matthews over. She produced reports that she said proved Lynne feared Noreen and what she might do.

She'd wanted Noreen arrested and made enough of a public outcry that the news media noticed, dug up the events from last year, which included the Amber Alert issued when Gia went missing, and reported on the shooting. Legal counsel for Dalton House filed a complaint, more to protect their reputation, Blake's attorney suspected, than to defend Lynne's. Despite the police report and eyewitnesses accounts that said Noreen had no choice but to shoot, the district attorney requested this hearing.

She picked at the cuticle on her left thumb. One grueling week had passed that Noreen spent at home. The hospital placed her on paid administrative leave pending the outcome of today's proceedings.

"Let's review what will happen when we walk into the courtroom. We are arguing that you fired your gun in self-defense. The district attorney will present the police officer's report regarding the events preceding the shooting. We have a copy of that statement, which clearly states Lynne Matthews was the aggressor and she failed to lower her weapon despite him ordering her to do so several times. Plus, we have his bodycam footage. The audio is garbled in some spots but it's clear she's threatening you. It picked up her confession about the fire. That in itself is sufficient to support our position."

Blake reached for and covered her hands, squeezing them reassuringly.

"There are," he paused to count the pages, "nine eyewitness statements, all asserting that Lynne Matthews leveled her weapon at you. A few of them were close enough to hear her threaten you."

He patted a thick binder. "These are the records from last year's events. The kidnapping and fire. The court proceedings committing her to psychiatric rehabilitation. We have copies of the tapes from the parental visits with your daughter and supplemental reports from her social service worker. We also have a statement from the Juvenile Court judge who met with Argia. None of these reports reflect favorably on Lynne Matthews, her attitude toward you or Blake, or her plans."

He held up a stapled report. "We know what her plans were. This is a rather lengthy interview with the man who acted as her accomplice. In return for a sentence of community service, he answered every question we asked.

"We have witnesses on hand ready to testify if necessary. But once we present all of this to the court, I don't think there will be a question that the shooting was justified."

He rose. "If you're ready, we can walk across the street to the courthouse."

She wasn't ready.

Not for the camera clicks of the news media when she and Blake entered the courtroom. Not for the benches filled with her co-workers, a handful of police officers in uniform, and more than two dozen firefighters. Gripping Blake's hand, she eyed the second row as she passed it. Blake's mom and sister were there, sitting beside her sister and brother-in-law, all of them grim faced.

In the first row, Kelly and Adam sat with Brittni and Joe. Argia, Mr. Dog and Mr. Fox were tucked between the two women.

She hadn't wanted Gia to be here but her questions this past week had been endless. Where was Mother? Was Noreen certain she could live forever with her and Daddy? Did the Angels let Mother into heaven? She thought only nice people went to heaven.

Blake thought it was important for Argia to be here for both their sakes.

Noreen pressed a tissue to her bleeding thumb. The microphone sat close to the judge's face and every breath he inhaled and exhaled resounded through the silent courtroom. The district attorney presented the facts of the case. Her attorney presented his evidence.

No one made a sound while the judge flipped through the pages of all the reports, his breath bouncing off all four corners of the room. Noreen's heart pounded in her ears. Her head throbbed.

And then it was over. Self defense. No charges to be filed.

"Ms. Jensen, you're free to go."

The room exploded with applause and she burst into tears. Blake crushed her to him, his eyes wet with tears. Against his chest, she saw her friends and family wiping their eyes. And she saw Gia, standing on the bench seat, her beloved stuffed animals pressed to her chest, grinning a toothy grin and clapping. This was the child who changed her life. The one she almost died to save. The one she killed for.

With Blake's arms around her, she walked to the bar separating the spectators from the attorneys. Gia jumped into her arms.

"Is it over, Weenie? Can we go home now forever?"

Noreen turned liquid eyes on Blake, and he lowered his mouth to hers for a sweet kiss. "I love you, Miss Jensen. And my daughter loves you, don't you Gia?" Her curls bounced in definite agreement. He squeezed her waist and caressed his daughter's cheek. "Are you ready to come home with us?"

She was too choked up to speak. She nodded.

Blake reached to take his daughter in his arms.

"We can go home now, Peanut, but it's not over. It's just beginning."

The End

CURIOUS TO KNOW...

Curious to know how it all started?
Loving Gia To Death
Available on Amazon and other e-tailers.

LOVING GIA TO DEATH
CHAPTER 1

The 9-1-1 emergency call from his home address sent chills down his back like nails scraping against a chalkboard. Lieutenant Blake Matthews jerked out of his chair so forcefully, it crashed backward with a loud bang.

When on duty, he listened but didn't actually hear the near constant sounds that reverberated through the fire station every day. The radio transmissions faded into the background as white noise until Station Twelve's distinctive two-level tones sounded. Then, just like every man's in the fire station, his ears perked up.

He sat elbow deep in training manuals and spreadsheets, designing a new special ops rescue program for the team when the tones cut through his concentration, and crimped his heart. Before he reached the door to exit the training room, a younger firefighter wrenched it open.

"Go!" he ordered. "I'll call someone in to cover for you ASAP."

Technically, leaving his post without being summoned to the emergency on board the back-up ladder truck or other supplemental fire equipment was a violation of protocol and grounds for suspension. But he wasn't worried. The unwritten rule in Station Twelve, and he presumed any fire department in the country, was that when it involved family, you dropped everything and took off. Your team would have your back, no questions asked.

He lived with these men twenty-four hours a day, every third day, and they were his family too, as much as the daughter he'd created. No one ate, slept, and risked their lives for strangers without forming an impenetrable bond with the man on his right and left side and the squad watching his six. What affected one of them touched all of them.

He raced to his personal truck, barely hearing someone yell from the building to keep them apprised. By now, the ambulance had reached his daughter so he listened to the radio transmissions to decide if he should rush to the house or head to the hospital.

Uncontrolled nausea? How could that be? He'd spent the day with Gia yesterday and she was fine. Laughing that little girl laugh that melted his heart. Sitting on his lap playing a game on his phone. Turning that angel face up to him to cajole him into buying three new frilly headbands instead of two, which was his quantity rule. Hell, she could convince him to buy out the whole store if she tried hard enough. Nothing was too good for his baby girl. And today she was sick enough to require an ambulance? He couldn't fathom it.

He picked up on the paramedics' transmission. They were transporting Gia to Children's Hospital. He'd be waiting.

Paramedic Joe Lystle jumped to his feet when the shrill emergency tone sounded, instinctively listening for the medical details bouncing off every corner of the firehouse. He ran to the ambulance, his half-eaten sandwich forgotten.

"Not again," he snapped. "When is he going to see it? And stop it, for crissake?"

A five-year-old reportedly convulsing, throwing up nonstop when her panicked mother dialed 9-1-1, the dispatcher relayed. But this wasn't merely any five-year old. This was Argia, the lieutenant's daughter.

Joe and his partner, Rob Yarnell, strapped on their gear with lightning speed while the dispatcher disclosed more specifics about the child's emergency. Uncontrolled nausea. Dehydration. Transport to the hospital STAT.

He cursed and activated the siren.

Rob stomped the gas pedal so hard, the ambulance jerked into motion. "This could be the real thing, Joe. We don't know."

"Dammit, Rob. We know."

Any emergency call automatically spikes a first responder's adrenaline, but when the victim is family, as all members of Deep Creek Fire Station Twelve were to each other, the need to arrive sooner becomes imperative. He mimicked the action when Rob floored the gas.

"We need a sit-down, Joe, that's what I say. It's gonna have to be me. He's gonna be pissed and argue with us. It'll be hard for him to hear but I don't think he'll be mad enough to take a swing at me. If he does, I hope I duck in time. I've seen what he lifts in the weight room."

He nodded and leaned forward in his seat, as if that helped shove the traffic in front of the ambulance out of their way. "Yeah, he'll be mad. He's the classic example of love being blind. But he knows we care about Argia like she was our own. Still, we'll be stepping out of bounds if we tell him what we think."

The ambulance screeched to a halt in front of Blake Matthews' driveway, automatically attracting a crowd of onlookers who spilled out onto their front porches. Joe looked around while he yanked the emergency equipment from the rear ambulance compartment. Why were so many people at home in the middle of the day?

Lynne Matthews burst out of her front door screaming for them to hurry. He braced himself for another irate interaction with the woman. They'd had them before. Just looking at her nauseated him. She splayed her hands against the sides of her face.

"What the hell took you so long?" Her right arm extended toward the house, her finger pointing inside. "My baby's in there choking to death. Can't you move any faster?"

Then she straightened and surveyed the street, assessing which neighbors watched and appeared concerned about her emergency. He rolled his eyes when she tugged on the deep V-neck midriff shirt she wore, purposefully offering an ample display of her assets. She was proud of her gifts. Considering her flare for drama, the woman should've been an actress. Especially since she now spoke as if she were center stage.

"I've never seen a child so sick before. It was all I could do to keep her hydrated. And she just kept clutching to me for dear life." She made this announcement to no one in particular. "If something happens to my darling baby, I don't think I could deal with it."

"Oh, brother," he whispered under his breath as they bypassed her and rushed into the house.

After eight years on the job, Blake knew the staff in the emergency room by their first names and he nodded a silent greeting to each one he passed. Likely they'd been informed already of the incoming transport. He snagged a cup of coffee from the EMT hospitality room and paced at the emergency entrance, barely sipping the brew. In minutes, the ambulance arrived. He ran to the rear and waited for Rob and Joe to open the doors.

Gia sat upright on the cot, an oxygen hose clipped to her

nose. Nevertheless, her face erupted into a wide smile. "Daddy!"

Perched beside her, his ex-wife scowled. He stepped out of the way while Rob and Joe rolled the cot out of the ambulance, his anxiety allayed by Gia's pink cheeks and cheerful greeting. They whisked her toward the emergency doors and he turned to follow when Lynne called out to him.

"Really, Blake. Would you at least help me out of this box?"

Her hand stretched toward him in anticipation of his assistance. He fleetingly entertained the urge to leave it hanging there and walk away but his mother raised him better. He respected women and treated them accordingly. Even though his mother wasn't a fan of The Captain, Lynne's self-created position in their life, his mom would expect him to be courteous. He reached for Lynne's hand, eyeing the red high heels and mini skirt. There was a time when an outfit like that would motivate him to crawl into the ambulance with her and lock the doors behind him. But not anymore.

Seductively, she placed both hands on his shoulders and shoved her breasts in his face when she jumped out of the ambulance. Before she could speak, he released himself from her grip and ran double-time toward the emergency doors.

Rob and Joe stood at the counter completing intake paper-work. Joe directed him to the cubicle where they'd rolled Gia's gurney.

The minute he threw back the curtain and reached her bed, Gia jumped to her feet and launched herself into his arms, causing the oxygen line to snap out of her nose and an intra-venous pole to roll forward when the line tugged.

"Daddy!" Her arms wrapped around his neck, a feeling he long ago decided he'd never tire of.

Blake hugged her and then, with his hands on her arms, eased her backward. "Hey, Peanut. What's up? Are you sick?"

Behind him, Lynne's high-pitched response pierced the air

and immediately, Gia's smile disappeared. "Of course she's sick. Why else would I summon an ambulance? She's been puking all over the house. It's been a helluva mess for me to clean up, I'll tell you that. By myself no less."

He ignored her and gazed into his little girl's eyes. "Honey, tell me where it hurts."

Wide-eyed, Gia plopped to the bed, crossing her legs Indian style. Her gaze dropped to a spot on the blanket. "I'm all better now, Daddy. It's okay."

Blake cupped his daughter's chin, the skin beneath his hand as soft as flannel. Was it?

Loving Gia To Death is also available on Amazon and other e-tailers.

MORE FROM RENA KOONTZ

OFF THE GRID FOR LOVE

BROKEN JUSTICE, BLIND LOVE

CRYSTAL CLEAR LOVE

The kindest thing you can do for an author is leave a review.

CPSIA information can be obtained
at www.ICGtesting.com
Printed in the USA
BVHW041107121221
623852BV00024B/1209